Laws of Elysium

by Jason Carl and Shane DeFreest

Laws of Elysium

Credits

Written by: Jason Carl and Shane DeFreest
Additional writing by: Cynthia Summers, Richard E. Dansky and Jess Heinig
Development by: Richard E. Dansky and Cynthia Summers
Additional development by: Jess Heinig
Editing by: Janice Sellers
Additional editing by: Alison Sturms
Previously published material has appeared in: Vampire: The Masquerade, Laws of the Night, Masquerade Second Edition, Masquerade Players Kit, Antagonists and Elysium: The Elder Wars
Art Direction by: Lawrence Snelly
Cover design, Layout and typesetting by: Katie McCaskill
Photography by: Jonathan Rhea
Models: Trevor Black, Chris Bell, Alissa Blitzer, Daniel Cameron, Shanti Faber, Charles J. Liggera, Stefani McClure, Wilson R. Nash, Mark Eric Stein, Riki Beth Stein, Raphael Sutton, Nukilwa "Nick" Taquilaya II, Nancy Vinick, David M. Wilson.
Costumer: Shanti Fader
Playtesters: The Coterie of the Silent Voice Playtest Team: Marc "Spence" Spencer, Tori Mauslein, Geoff Hinkle, David Blackwell, Mykle McGovern, Tom Willis, Marisa Stanley, David Cole, Mike Metcalf, Shannon Cass, Pamela Lord, Mike Curnutt, Chris Arnold, Sally Arnold, Julian Dillard, Tim Dawson, Brian Gates, Misty Gates, James Holman, Trevor Hoyle, Stephanie Hoyle, Mike Chambers, Robert Hinkle and David Flannery. Whew!

Special Thanks To:

Mike Schatz and Stephe Herman for rules consultation, Issac Aden, Peter Bossio, Shanti Fader, Charles J. Liggera, Stefani McClure, Tara Marlowe, Maceo Marquez, Wilson R. Nash, Raphael Sutton and Nancy Vinick for modeling, Shanti Fade for costuming and Mark Scibelli for assisting in finding locations on **The Shining Host.**

735 PARK NORTH BLVD.
SUITE 128
CLARKSTON, GA 30021
USA

© 1998 White Wolf Publishing, Inc. All rights reserved. Reproduction without the written permission of the publisher is expressly forbidden, except for the purposes of reviews, and for blank character sheets, which may be reproduced for personal use only. White Wolf, Vampire the Masquerade, Vampire the Dark Ages, World of Darkness and Mage the Ascension are registered trademarks of White Wolf Publishing, Inc. All rights reserved. Werewolf the Apocalypse, Wraith the Oblivion, Changeling the Dreaming, Werewolf the Wild West, Trinity, Laws of Elysium, Elysium The Elder Wars, Laws of the Night, Antagonists, Masquerade Second Edition, Liber des Goules the Book of Ghouls, The Shining Host, Laws of the Wild and The Long Night are trademarks of White Wolf Publishing, Inc. All rights reserved. All characters, names, places and text herein are copyrighted by White Wolf Publishing, Inc.

The mention of or reference to any company or product in these pages is not a challenge to the trademark or copyright concerned.

This book uses the supernatural for settings, characters and themes. All mystical and supernatural elements are fiction and intended for entertainment purposes only. Reader discretion is advised.

Check out White Wolf online at
http://www.white-wolf.com; alt.games.whitewolf and rec.games.frp.storyteller
PRINTED IN USA.

Contents

Table of Contents

Just Visiting: A Cautionary Tale	4
Introduction	10
Character Creation	16
Disciplines and Rituals	38
Playing An Elder	58
Storytelling for Elders	94
Appendix: New Rules and Clarifications	144

Just Visiting: A Cautionary Tale

I have been in Elysium for two hours, and no fewer than four ill-mannered Toreador brats have introduced themselves to me — without benefit of formal introduction. Each came up, smiled his or her most puppetlike smile, and then announced who he or she was — as if I knew or cared. Then each in turn got miffed when I refused to reciprocate or (more importantly) preen and wiggle to be introduced to an artist of such *devastating* beauty and importance.

They fail to understand that I have no interest in who they are, what they do, or what favors they want from me in return for the grace of their presence. When you have watched over Rembrandt's shoulder as he painted "The Night Watch," the childish scribblings these moderns try to perpetrate as art upon an unsuspecting populace...let me simply say that they leave something to be desired. Such is the curse of America — there's not a city on this continent older than I am, and these home-grown Kindred have no sense of style or of history. They've seen a century and think that makes them "elders." Any one of them who's outlived his mortal family feels entitled to whine about the agony of his endless existence.

I've buried empires in my day. These children are pathetic.

I turn and wander through the museum. The collection is fairly impressive — the pre-Raphaelite collection is displayed well, if a bit unimaginatively, and the more modern pieces are banished to side galleries. I must grant the Americans that. They may not have any class of their own, but they know enough to buy it when they can.

A few more twists and turns, and I find myself in the room where the prince of this city holds his court. He is a tall man, with high cheekbones and a severe haircut, and I see him surrounded by his childer and advisors as he gravely nods at the tale of some ragamuffin neonate in an ill-fitting suit. There is nothing important going on here, just a shadow-show of the way in which princedom was formulated a half-millennium ago.

Eventually, the neonate finishes, the prince waves his hand, and the hangers-on applaud politely at this display of princely justice. I have no idea what just went on, nor do I care. I am here on business. I step forward. "Your Majesty," I say, knowing full well that this creature whom I must present myself to is at least three centuries younger than I. He looks up at me, a bit astonished at the "interruption." Various of his ghouls and retainers move to place themselves between him and myself, as if that would make a difference were I to wish His Majesty harm.

"I wish to present myself to you, and request permission to dwell in your city, in accordance with our Traditions," I hear myself saying by rote. I helped to draft those Traditions, once upon a time.

"We appreciate your adherence to those Traditions," is his response, and internally I cringe. Not another American who's adopted and abused the royal "we," please — it's another case of aping form, not function. "Your name and business in our domain?" The toadies and harpies around him lean forward, anxious to be the first with tidbits of gossip about my arrival. One, I can see, has been so rude as to look at my aura — her eyes are wide in shock, and she's taken a step or two backward. It's a pity, really; she's a pretty little thing, though suffering from that plague of fashion that says all of our kind must wear black lace in some form or other.

I smile at her before I introduce myself, small acts of sadism being one of the few pleasures I still permit myself. "Of course, Your Majesty. I am called Alaric Montfleury, at least in these days, and my business in your city is strictly personal."

A Cautionary Tale

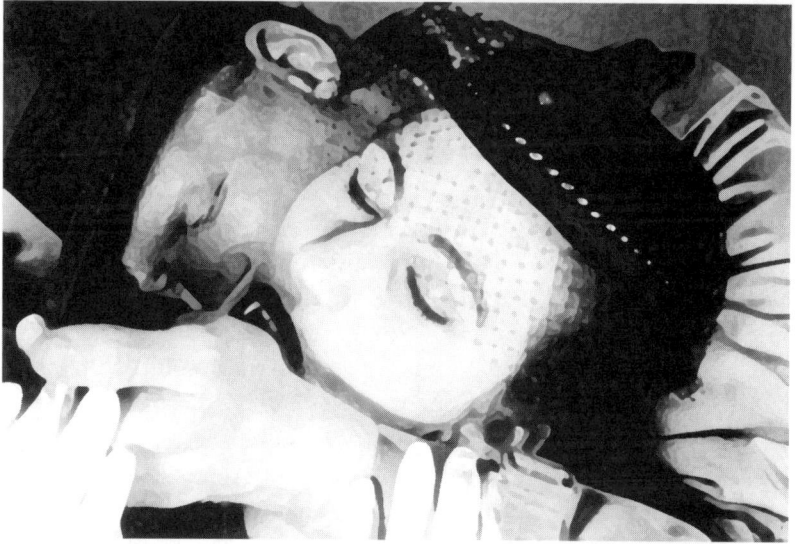

The prince leans forward and scrunches up his face in that way that seems to indicate deep concentration to the younger generations. "Montfleury? We seem to recall that name."

"Of course you do, Your Majesty. Your sire must have told you stories about learning the odd bit of statecraft from my humble self, in addition to his sire. Your grandsire and I spent several years together at Montségur, watching the Cathar experiment play itself out." He's not listening. I smile. He, and one by one his court after him, have realized exactly what stands in front of them.

"Of course," he finally stammers after a few seconds of silence. The woman, who was swifter on the uptake than the others, turns and hurries out of the room, her footfalls clattering in the emptiness. "I…we welcome you to our domain, trust that you will abide by the Traditions, and hope to have your company at future Elysiums. Until then…." He lets the sentence trail off. I nod, and smile, and bow from the neck as I turn and walk out.

It's simple, really. My words were inconsequential — a reference to my age and history, and His Majesty's place (inconsequential) relative to all that. What I really told him was, "I can take this city away from you any time I wish, and both you and I know it. I have no intention of doing so, mind you — if I wanted a city, it wouldn't be this huddled collection of pollution-stained towers on the shores of a stinking and frozen lake. This is merely a visit, a brief stop as I head westward toward a city more worthy of my effort."

Laws of Elysium

As I turn the corner back toward the museum's front entrance, I hear footsteps. It is the pretty young woman, of course. I expected as much.

"What is your real purpose here?" she asks. She is very young and very new to the blood, and terribly serious. "There can't be anything here that you want."

I shrug and look her up and down, then say, "Perhaps." She blushes a bit, and I find myself vaguely disappointed in her distinct lack of self-control. "But really, I'm just passing through, and I wanted to make sure I followed the Traditions to the letter so as not to cause Prince Michael any undue stress." It's near enough to the absolute truth as to make no difference, not that she will ever believe me.

She laughs humorlessly. "I'm sure your presence is a great comfort to him. In the meantime, is there anything I can do to make your stay here more pleasant?" *Or more brief*, I can hear her think.

"No, nothing at all," I reply. "I thank you for your pains, though. Now if you'll excuse me?" She curtsies and steps out of my way, and I continue on toward the door. Behind me the whispers are already starting, as I knew they would.

He's here to take the princedom.... He's going to support Michael and wipe out any opposition.... He's actually an archon here to cleanse the city.... There are other elders coming.... He's a diabolist.... He mentioned the Cathars so he must be Sabbat.... He's really Michael's grandsire.... I didn't see his reflection in the glass, so he must be Lasombra antitribu.... *He's going to kill us all....*

As the doors swing shut behind me (no ghoul doormen, a bad sign, that) I laugh softly to myself. All the little vampires are now scrambling to recalculate their petty plots, trying to imagine where I fit into their equations. All of the conspiracies will unwind themselves and recombine, murders will be committed, bodies will vanish, and generally everything will go to hell in a handbasket because the nice neat little picture the local Cainites have painted for themselves has just been shattered. Parochialism never pays, not among our kind, and these children are about to learn that lesson the hard way.

It shouldn't take long for the firestorm to flare up and burn itself out. The survivors will be smarter, faster and more cunning than they are now, and the fat with which Michael's surrounded himself will be trimmed away. I won't be surprised if Michael himself goes. His grandsire will be disappointed, no doubt, but has grown inured to those kinds of losses over the centuries.

A Cautionary Tale

I could be mistaken, of course. Perhaps the conspirators will show some sense and relax. Perhaps they'll keep my presence in perspective, or want to tippy-toe in my presence so as not to arouse the dread anger of the ancient vampire. Perhaps, for once, they'll behave.

I hear a scream behind me, and the sound of broken glass. Perhaps not, after all.

Introduction

Do you know what it's like to live forever? To watch history pass before you as a pageant of color and noise that fades to darkness and silence when you recall it? To fear the uncertain future promised by today's youth, and to dream of past glories? To rendezvous with an old lover every few decades or to spend a century preparing to confront a rival for a crime that occurred two millennia ago?

The elders of the Kindred not only know, they have lived it. For countless years they have existed, watching civilizations rise and fall, measuring their lifespans by eras of human history. Their power over the night and Kindred society is something that many vampires envy, but only the foolish would reach for it. Such is the privilege of surviving the centuries.

This book outlines elders for **The Masquerade**, what a player should be ready for, and what a Storyteller needs. From rules to character creation to storytelling, there is plenty here to use and abuse.

Mind's Eye Theatre

We've all been playing **Mind's Eye Theatre** in some way, long before we had a name for it. Instead of vampires, we were cowboys and Indians, or cops and robbers. In essence, it's a game of make-believe, but one with very specific parameters of time and place. In that make-believe, players interact with each other as characters, assisted by a few rules to help them resolve conflicts.

Mind's Eye Theatre is about telling a story. The Storyteller creates the framework of the plot, then turns the players loose to watch them create a story of that plot. In between, there are shifting alliances, vagaries of circumstance, conflicts and consequences. It is not a story about a goal, but how that goal was reached.

The Elders

An elder is simply defined as a vampire who has managed to survive for at least 250 years. Such a short definition does not, however, cover the many requirements the elders demand before one is allowed to sit at their table. It takes strength, resources and cunning to arrive at the coveted title of "elder"; age is no longer the sole prerequisite.

The Camarilla was founded on the will of the elders, and even now they continue as its strongest proponents and leaders. It is elders who make up the upper ranks of the Inner Circle and Justicars, and often some of the most powerful princes. Yet they are also the favored pawns of the Methuselahs in their unending Jyhad. In the Sabbat, the elders are the bishops and paladins, feared by the younger ranks, for only the strongest can survive to such age. Their fanaticism and callousness can give even the most experienced crusaders pause; no one crosses them once and lives to boast of it. Yet they are well aware that the Anarch Revolt was started because of elders who overstepped their bounds, and that their youth watch them now for the first signs that another revolt may be due.

Elders are often thrown into a chronicle with little preparation, usually seen as just one more type of vampire at Elysium. They may

Introduction

know a few more things, happen to be a little older, and have a few more nifty tricks up their black sleeves, but they're still just like every other vampire in a chronicle, right? Yes and no. Elders do know a few more things that most vampires, they are a little older than the average vampire in a story, and they have plenty of interesting aces to play. What both players and Storytellers tend to forget is the impact that elders can have on a chronicle, and that elders have been around far too long to be classified as merely "old bloodsuckers."

An elder's appearance can easily throw a chronicle into a tizzy, even if she doesn't directly affect the action. Why is she here? What does she want? Does her presence bode good or ill? Her age and experience will draw many younger vampires into her sphere, hoping for favorable attention or assistance with a particular quandary. She will be in turn affected by her extremely long unlife, often unable to adapt to new technology, bearing long grudges and hatreds, and cursed as the only emotions left to her become hate, rage and bitterness.

How to Use This Book

Elder characters are not meant for new, inexperienced or immature players. These creatures are centuries old, and require more thought and time than the average vampire. Their mere presence can unbalance a chronicle if they're simply thrown in without thought, and immature players can run roughshod over the story and other players simply by dint of their enhanced abilities. This book is meant to prepare both Storytellers and would-be players for the challenges of elder characters.

The Only Rules That Matter

Behave yourself so everyone can enjoy the game. These are meant to keep players safe and non-players happy. If you're playing an elder, you should be able to recite these like the Traditions. If you can't remember either, you're not ready for this.

#1-It's Only a Game

If your character is embarrassed by a peer, a plot falls apart, a rival wins the day — it's just a game. Don't take things too seriously, as that will spoil not only your fun, but also the fun of everyone around you.

Laws of Elysium

Leave the game behind when it ends. It's one thing to hold an impromptu salon at a friend's house to complain about the prince, but calling your fellow elders at four in the morning to discuss Gehenna takes things a little too far. Keep some perspective.

#2-No Touching

Never actually have physical contact with another player. No matter how careful you are. Accidents happen. Use your imagination and the rules to cover physical logistics.

#3-No Stunts

Never climb, jump, run, leap or swing from anything during a game. Keep the action in "live action" low-key. If you can imagine yourself as a millennia-old bloodsucking creature of the night, then you can certainly imagine yourself to be running when you're actually walking.

#4-No Weapons

Fake or real weapons of any sort are forbidden. Even obviously silly toy weapons are not allowed. Such props could give people the wrong impression as to what you're doing, and in the dark could conceivably be mistaken for the real thing. Swords and other sharp pointy things found in catalogs or at Renaissance fairs look real enough to worry bystanders, even if they are peace-bound. No matter how well a sword fits your character's persona, leave the stuff at home. Use item cards to represent weapons instead.

#5-No Drugs or Drinking

This one is (or should be) a real no-brainer. Drugs and alcohol do not create peak performance. They reduce your ability to think and react, meaning that, among other things, your roleplaying ability will be impaired. Players impaired by drugs and alcohol are a danger to other players and to the game. There's nothing wrong with *playing* a character who's drunk or tripping from some tainted blood, but actually bringing such stuff to a game is in bad taste at worst, illegal at best. Don't do it.

#6-Be Mindful of Others

Remember, not everyone you see, or who sees you, will be playing the game. A game can be unnerving, even frightening, to passersby. Be considerate of nonplayers in your vicinity, and make sure that if you are in a public area, your gameplay actions are not going to alarm anyone. Stay alert to your surroundings, and be ready to drop character if nonplayers start to take notice. Trying to explain to the local security that you're not *really* hunting an unfortunate mortal as part of a midnight salon is an exercise in futility. In fact, if you can warn your local police force and merchants about what you're doing before you start playing, they may be a bit more sympathetic to your presence.

#7-The Rules Are Flexible

Feel free to ignore or adjust any of the rules in this book if it will make your game better. We at White Wolf call this "The Golden Rule." If some rule included in this book (beyond the ones listed here) doesn't work for your troupe, change it. But be consistent and fair. Nobody likes rules that change every week nor "no-win" scenarios. If your troupe finds a new way to handle, say, a certain Tremere ritual that works better for you than the one in this book, go for it. The idea is to have fun.

#8-Have Fun

Not "Win." Not "Go out and kill everyone else." Just "Have fun." The object of the game is not to win. In fact there are no rules for "winning." The goal is to tell great stories, not to achieve superiority over the other players. The game is not about the goal, but about the journey to get to the goal and what happens along the way.

Character Creation

Warning

This is a quick-and-dirty guide to elder creation. We assume you are already familiar with the **Mind's Eye Theatre** character creation process from **The Masquerade Second Edition** or **Laws of the Night**. If you aren't, read through the process in either **Masquerade Second Edition** or **Laws of the Night** before you plunge in here.

Any lists of Traits, Abilities, Disciplines, or Merits and Flaws not included here can be found in **Laws of the Night**.

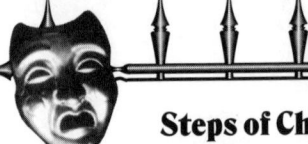

Laws of Elysium

Steps of Character Creation

Step One: Inspiration — Who are you?
— Choose your clan
— Choose your Nature and Demeanor

Step Two: Attributes — What are your basic capabilities?
— Prioritize Attributes (10/8/6)
— Choose Traits

Step Three: Advantages — What do you know?
— Choose Abilities (8)
— Choose Disciplines (6)
— Choose Influences (6)

Step Four: Last Touches — Fill in the details
— Assign Blood Traits
— Assign Willpower Traits
— Choose Beast/Path Traits (Sabbat members must choose a Path)
— Record Status Traits
— Choose Negative Traits

Step Five: Spark of Life — Narrative descriptions and Extra Traits at Storyteller discretion

Step One: Inspiration – Who are you?

There's a lot to consider when playing an elder, not the least of which is what makes your character something more than a walking, blood-drinking relic. Don't think just yet about all the historic events she's witnessed. Think about who she was before she was Embraced, how long she's been a vampire, and how unlife has changed her over the years. Find something that you, the player, can identify with in your character. What's so exciting about her that you would want to *be* her for the evening, much less a thousand years?

Remember that many of your character's attitudes may have crystallized when she was Embraced. No doubt she has changed little over the years, and she'll be glad to tell you that such adherence to her beliefs has served her well over the centuries. Think about when your character was Embraced, how she felt about certain ideas, and how time has battered at those ideals.

Lastly, think a little about what she was before her change and afterward. Let questions like these fuel the creative process and spark something new and different for you. Was she a peasant or a noble? How educated was she? Was the Embrace an unwelcome change, or did it empower her? How did her sire treat her? Are there friendships and interests that she has maintained for all these years, and if so, how? Does she have a paramour she has a rendezvous with in Paris every five years, or has she given up on love since her mortal mate passed on? How many childer has she sired? Think of three events that marked turning points in her unlife (for better or worse), and how did she take the changes?

The Name Game

When creating an elder character, it will certainly behoove you in the long run to put a little thought into her name. After all, you're going to be hearing it for quite a while, and an unwise choice will have you cringing when your name is called.

Names like "Slash," "Blade," "Desire" and the like are fine for neonates, but the average vampire on the street isn't likely to know the difference between "Blade, Brujah neonate" and "Blade, elder of Clan Toreador." If such a thing would bother your elder considerably, then spare the other characters your continual wrath, and choose again. Those elders who can afford to keep single names are usually high enough in the power structure that it doesn't much matter, or their names have certain attachments that make them impossible to mistake. Examples of these include Rebekah (the Monitor of Chicago), Democritus (the Ventrue Justicar) or Critias (elder of Clan Brujah).

Consider the following factors: How old is your character? What is her heritage? Where is she from? What were her parents' names? Were there circumstances when it was necessary for her to change her name (such as coming through Ellis Island, or to avoid harassment)?

Baby name books are excellent resources to find variations on John and Mary (or Ian and Maire, or Jean and Marie). Look for those that list ethnic equivalents and the country of origin. For last names, the telephone book makes a good start if you have an idea of what you want. If you need help, some research may be in order. It looks a little silly to have your proud Italian Toreador announce himself as "Giovanni Jones."

Choose Your Clan

Your choice of clan in many ways determines what sort of unlife your character can look forward to, and how he might spend his old age. It is possible to be Caitiff (that is, clanless), but such elders are frequently scorned by their "clannish" brethren. See **Laws of the Night**, Chapter Two, for complete descriptions about the clans available.

Choose Nature and Demeanor

Your Nature is your character's true self, often hidden under many protective layers. Your Demeanor is the face you show most often to the world, particularly when dealing with people. A character's Nature and Demeanor can be wildly different, similar, or even the same, though few people (much less, elder vampires) are so open. A complete listing of possible Natures and Demeanors can be found in **Laws of the Night**.

Step Two: Attributes

Attributes describe everything a character naturally is. Are you strong? Are you brave? Are you persuasive? Questions such as these are answered in your choice of Attributes. Attribute Traits use adjectives to describe a character in the same way that adjectives describe a character in a book. So the Nosferatu elder who rescued his favorite ghoul from a witch-hunter might be *Energetic, Ferocious* and *Determined*, while the Ventrue who is currently attempting to outmaneuver a Tremere for control of a television station might be *Clever, Cunning* and *Shrewd*.

Unlike a regular vampire character, elders' categories fall as 10 Primary, eight Secondary and six Tertiary.

Step Three: Advantages

Abilities

These represent your abilities beyond the outline provided in Attributes. This is what you can do and what you've learned, rather than who you are. Abilities let you perform specialized tasks that are only possible with training — translating another language, understanding an occult text, working a computer. Elder characters begin with eight Abilities. A full listing of these Traits can be found in **Laws of the Night**.

Disciplines

These are the vampiric powers available to all undead. Elders may begin with six Disciplines, but you must spend Negative Traits to take out-of-clan Disciplines (one per level of out-of-clan). Some Disciplines may not be available, or may require special penalties. Check with your Storyteller before taking anything you're not 100 percent certain about.

Influences

This reflects your elder's control over mortal society. Over time, such control can grow to amazing proportions, making elders truly formidable opponents in the Jyhad, and one reason why they are frequently unopposed. Few are likely to interfere with someone who could quite possibly call heads of state and military leaders to assist her.

How many Influences you begin with should be the purview of your Storyteller; six makes a good starting point. Long-time players being moved into the elder arena may start to purchase their Influences from the lists given. The Influences listed here are from level six and up; lower levels may be found in **Laws of the Night**.

Step Four: Last Touches

Fill in the last details, including Status, generation and Willpower.

Generation

Your Storyteller will quite possibly have a target generation in mind for your character, and may request that you not buy down your generation with Negative Traits. Elders generally are of the eighth generation, although the Pretenders attempt to presume eldership at ninth.

Status

It is safe to assume that most elders have at least two Status Traits: *Acknowledged* and *Respected* to start with. Any more will be a matter for your Storyteller to decide.

Willpower and Blood Traits

See **Laws of the Night** for the starting number of Willpower and Blood Traits available to your generation.

Laws of Elysium

Beast/Path Traits

It is an unfortunate fact that as a vampire ages, his grip on the Beast can grow weaker. Many find themselves struggling nightly to maintain the facade of order both in their surroundings and in their souls. Whether Sabbat or Camarilla, a vampire who's a ravening monster is a danger to those around her as well as to herself. At five Beast Traits, the character descends into permanent frenzy, and will most likely be put down like a rabid animal.

Elder characters begin with two Beast/Path Traits. You may take another Beast Trait for two Negative Traits, but remember that it will now take only two more Beast Traits to fall into the final frenzy.

Step Five: Spark of Life

Like any other vampire character, your elder needs to be fully described, putting a little flesh on the bare bones of Traits and Influences. Otherwise, your character is just a cardboard cut-out with some nifty tricks.

• Background Story — So, what have you been up to all these years? When was your character Embraced, and what did she do before then? What events in history has she witnessed, and how did they affect her?

• Motivations — Something must be driving her through these last days. What is it? Is she attempting to escape the machinations of a Methuselah? Is she searching for Golconda? Does she thirst for revenge against the Kindred who slew her childer? Whether it's hate, revenge, fear or hope, your elder's prime motivation will color her actions and often reflect on the game around you.

• Appearance — Has she chosen to ignore the fashion parade after so many decades, and prefers simple gowns reflective of medieval times? Does he still sport the muttonchops he wore when he rode at General Lee's side? Look for props and costuming that reflect your character's age and outlook as well as her Traits.

• Equipment — Talk with a Storyteller about the kinds of things you're likely to start play with. She is, of course, perfectly within her rights to disallow LAW rockets, tanks or original Rembrandts.

• Quirks — Everyone has little tricks and peccadilloes that make him unique, such as a favorite curse word, a method of donning a hat or the way he relieves stress. In the case of elders, these quirks deepen over time, and may be leftover habits from other times. When you consider your quirks, think about how and why you started doing such things. If your elder refuses to exit a car until she's looked in the rearview mirror for an all-clear, consider that she was perhaps attacked when she got out of a carriage one night in the late 18th century, and she has never been careless about such since. Think about habits she might have picked up over the years, and why. Such quirks can be good roleplaying aids, and they can establish character more effectively than a name tag and a few challenges.

Sample Character Creation

Michael has been playing a vampire in **MET** for some time, and has come a long way as a roleplayer since those first days as a neonate. His Storyteller, Laura, thinks he's ready for a challenge and is mature enough to handle the responsibility — she offers him the role of an elder. All she asks is that he keep in mind the sort of game she's running when he creates the character. Michael asks Laura if there's anything in particular she's looking for in this elder. While she can't tell him everything she has planned (it would ruin the surprise), she does request that the character be a sort who could serve in an advisory capacity and occasionally do some "Deep Throat" duty. With a clear goal before him, Michael starts working on fleshing out some early skeletal ideas.

Laura's game is primarily Camarilla-based with a number of mortals. The mood is largely one of mystery and conspiracy, with an *X-Files* sort of theme. Several plots are in the works, but two storylines have begun to stagnate. The presence of an elder would hopefully jump-start them again. A Sabbat elder would shake things up too much, and Laura doesn't want to take her chronicle down that path. Michael debates an independent clan, but he decides otherwise when he can't find a reason why such a character would appear in a Camarilla town. Finally, he chooses to make his elder a Ventrue, a clan he's never played before. He decides that the elder was a student of the great philosophers and was Embraced during the Golden Age of Greece by a Cainite who wanted to tweak a rival. Over the years, the character has lived many lives and used many names; currently he goes by the name "Alexander Dent."

Alexander is, as he has always been, a seeker of wisdom, never satisfied with a single easy answer. He debates and deliberates on the

eternal questions of life, no matter what the era, and Michael thinks that Alexander's Nature is suggestive of a Visionary. Over the years, however, Alexander has learned that those who question are not always welcome, particularly in Cainite society, and he's learned the truth behind "Go along to get along." Michael decides that Alexander poses as a Traditionalist to keep princes and other nosy folks out of his personal business.

Michael prioritizes Alexander's Attributes as Mental, Physical and Social, and chooses Traits that would reflect someone who grew up in the city-state of Athens under the expectations of the times. For Alexander's Mental Traits, Michael chooses *Reflective*, *Wise*, *Insightful*, *Knowledgeable* and *Observant*, all Traits that would seem sensible for one who spent most of his years in thought and in various schools of philosophy. He decides *Rational* and *Calm* are Traits the Ventrue would have cultivated in Alexander. Realizing that there will be plenty of Mental Challenges, Michael takes *Disciplined*, *Attentive* and *Shrewd*, just in case someone gets an idea that Alexander's introspection means he's a pushover.

Next come Physical Traits. Alexander would have been expected to maintain physical fitness along with mental fitness, so Michael considers the Traits that would reflect someone who's fit, but not necessarily "buff." He eventually chooses *Athletic x2*, *Dexterous x2*, *Energetic x2*, *Resilient* and *Tenacious*. Michael decides that Alexander did all right for the times, but just all right.

Lastly come Social Traits. Alexander's been something of a loner (philosophical thinking does tend to be a one-person sport), and Michael thinks that Alex knows how to get along with people, but he isn't a glad-hander like many in his clan. Michael decides that Alexander is quite *Persuasive* and *Eloquent* from all the decades of debate. Alexander is also *Dignified* and *Commanding* when he needs to be and is *Friendly* with those he meets. After choosing what immediately sprang to mind, Michael isn't sure what else to take. He asks Laura for suggestions, and she looks over his choices so far. After hearing Alexander's sketchy story, she asks Michael if Alex would be the sort to pursue Golconda. Michael agrees, and decides to add *Compassionate*; Alex is slowly learning the ways of Golconda, and this indicates he has taken the first steps.

Now come Abilities. While it might be rare for a Ventrue to be without *Finance*, Michael can't imagine how a Greek philosophy student would have it. Michael thinks more about what Alex has

Character Creation

been doing all this time, and most recently, and decides that for the past five years Alex has been teaching evening Philosophy courses at a university. Laura approves the idea, seeing it as the basis for some interesting story hooks. Michael chooses *Performance: Debate* x2, then *Performance: Lecturing* (to make sure Alex's students don't fall asleep in class). He adds *Subterfuge* and *Kindred Lore* (Alex has been around long enough to learn something of the Sabbat and other vampires). Like it or not, Alex will be considered a leader among the youth of the clan, so Michael takes *Leadership*. Michael's fairly certain that Alex is fluent in several languages, but he can only afford two levels of *Linguistics* — his native Greek and Latin, which are both necessary for Classical studies.

For Disciplines, Michael decides that Alex would be far more likely to use *Presence* over *Dominate*, and buys *Presence* up through *Majesty*. He puts the last two levels in *Fortitude*.

Now it's time to buy Influences. As Alexander takes such a high interest in the educational system and spends so much time there, Michael takes four levels of *University* Influence. Michael adds a level of *High Society*, to reflect the various mortal circles Alex travels in as a professor. Lastly, unable to resist the pull, he takes a level of *Finance*. Because Alex is Ventrue as well, he automatically begins with a permanent *Finance* Influence Trait. Michael figures you just can't get away from some things, and decides that the *Finance* Influences were gifts from Alex's sire.

Laura requests that Alex go no higher than seventh generation. For now, he starts at eighth, but Michael thinks that someone as old as Alex should be at least a little lower — something to consider when Negative Traits are bought. He records Alex's Blood Traits and starting Willpower for an eighth-generation vampire. As Alex is not yet well-known in the city, his beginning Status Traits are *Acknowledged* and *Respected*.

As Alex is an elder, he begins with two Beast Traits. Michael chooses *Vigilante* and *Item* (crucifix). Alexander didn't handle the coming of Christianity too well, and the Inquisition left him with many bad memories.

Michael takes two Negative Traits, *Oblivious* (when Alex gets busy with a problem, he forgets to pay attention around him) and *Impatient* (particularly with dull students). These he uses to buy up Alex's generation to seventh, and he records Alex's Blood (9) and Willpower Traits (3).

Satisfied, Michael passes his sheet to Laura. She looks it over, and decides that some areas are a little sparse. She gives him a few extra Traits, and suggests that he take at least one level of *Dominate* and one level of *Occult* Ability. Alexander is going to be in the thick of a few things, and Laura wants him to be ready to come out swinging. Michael takes the Basic levels of *Dominate*, a single *Occult* and throws the last three points into Traits — one Physical (*Quick*), one Social (*Magnetic*) and one Mental (*Observant*). Laura approves Alexander's final incarnation, and Michael sits down to consider the rest of Alex's long story before joining play.

Influence

Obviously, these are much more powerful than the levels given in **Laws of the Night**. The Storyteller should feel free to disallow these if they would unbalance a game.

Bureaucracy

Cost	Desired Effect
7	Control over state bureaucrats (legislator, judge, etc.).
8	Utilize the resources of internal federal agencies — FBI, DEA, ATF, INS, etc.
9	Affect foreign policy; utilize the resources of the CIA; access the Secret Service.
10	You can affect change in national legislature and judiciary; you keep the president's number in your Rolodex.

Church

Cost	Desired Effect
8	You control a nationally known evangelist or organization of comparable stature.
9	You have access to the Society of Leopold or other Church-sponsored hunter groups; you have influence in a monastic order.
10	You have sway in a major sect.

Finance

Cost	Desired Effect
7	You own many businesses locally, and contribute greatly to the local economy.

8	You can affect the financial stability of other cities within 50 miles of your own.
9	You have the wealth and backing of a major corporation/Fortune 500 company; you own several businesses; Wall Street jumps when you sneeze.
10	You number among the richest people in the world.

Health

Cost	Desired Effect
6	You control an outpatient clinic/blood bank.
7	You control a major metropolitan hospital.
8	Access and manipulate most all local goings-on in the medical community.
9	Obtain national funding, drug research and cutting-edge medical information.
10	Discuss matters with the Surgeon General; influence in the World Health Organization.

High Society

Influence and notoriety in the mortal world at this level can be as much a curse as it is a blessing. It can border on a major breach of the Masquerade.

Cost	Desired Effect
6	Major local celebrity status.
7	The local social scene is completely malleable to your whims.
8	National celebrity status — you often get calls from major talk shows.
9	You're on guest lists across the country; part of the social scene of several cities.
10	International celebrity status.

Industry

Cost	Desired Effect
7	Organize major strikes.
8	Control at least one national union.
9	Arrange major "accidents," such as chemical leaks and factory fires; orchestrate a large-scale walk-out or factory recall.
10	Oil spills, chemical accidents, factory shutdowns — all in a night's work.

Laws of Elysium

Legal

Cost	Desired Effect
6	Control a city or circuit judge; can circumvent city court system.
7	Control a law firm; can circumvent state court system.
8	Oversee the parole board; arrange a governor's pardon; speed up a scheduled execution; can circumvent circuit court or federal court; may have sealed records opened.
9	Can have cases presented in the Supreme Court; access to federal court documents.
10	You can arrange a presidential pardon.

Media

Cost	Desired Effect
5	Kill small local articles or reports completely.
6	Broadcast fake stories (regionally).
7	Control a major metropolitan newspaper; have an editorial position.
8	Carry a White House press pass.
9	Manipulate the content of a nationally read magazine.
10	Broadcast fake stories (nationally); Rupert Murdoch, Ted Turner and you.

Occult

Cost	Desired Effect
7	Research Basic Ritual from other sect.
8	Research Intermediate Ritual from other sect; access a partial copy of *The Book of Nod*.
9	Research Advanced Ritual from other sect.
10	Access a near-complete version of *The Book of Nod*.

Police

Cost	Desired Effect
7	Instigate SWAT raids.
8	Get people extradited.
9	Have police chiefs replaced.
10	Complete control of the city police.

Politics

Cost	Desired Effect
9	Get your candidate in a major office; control Senate subcommittees.
10	You have people inside the Oval Office or the UN; influence diplomatic relations; can acquire diplomatic immunity.

Street

Cost	Desired Effect
6	Access large quantities of contraband.
7	Acquire automatic weapons.
8	Control all gang activity in the city.
9	Nothing happens on the street without you knowing about it.
10	You drew up the blueprints for the L.A. riots.

Transportation

Cost	Desired Effect
8	Can travel nationally without problems.
9	Shut down major airlines or cause serious delays for other travelers.
10	Travel internationally with almost no degree of risk.

Underworld

Cost	Desired Effect
6	Control local Mafia family.
7	Control a major money laundering operation ($3,000), drug cartel, pornography empire.
8	Have a word in most crime syndicates across the country.
9	Arrange high-level political assassinations.
10	Some international terrorists are under your control.

University

Cost	Desired Effect
7	Falsify a post-graduate degree.
8	Have faculty fired; assure tenure.
9	Close down school districts; affect curriculum statewide.
10	Complete control of curriculum, faculty and all records; falsify doctorate; seat on the Board of Regents.

Acquired Tastes

Even if they don't voice the concern, every elder fears the day when he must drink vampire blood to survive. While some diablenists may have begun such as a hobby, needing it to survive is much different than "recreational use."

Such degeneration is often tied to the loss of Humanity and to the changes wrought by age, but not always. Some millennia-old Kindred still drink (and prefer) mortal blood, while some relatively young vampires cannot drink from anyone but mortals. Storytellers should make such a change a story element, not one that automatically takes over in a single night. Of course, if the Storyteller fears wholesale slaughter if an elder develops a thirst for that vintage one can neither buy nor raise, she is perfectly within her rights to disallow it.

Below is a set of warning signs that a character may be sliding into cannibalism. If she meets several of these conditions, chances are that she will start with the occasional "nip off the top" until she can no longer drink anything but vampire blood.

- Diablerist
- Sire addicted to Kindred blood
- Three or more Beast Traits
- Sire is/was a diablerist
- Active for more than 500 years
- Has a Derangement related to blood and/or feeding
- Has sired a large number of childer (five or more)
- Has Blood Bound a number of younger vampires — especially one's own childer
- At odds with one's own sire
- Has almost no mortal Allies, friends or other ties
- Has any Nature but Architect, Caregiver, Cavalier or Martyr

Merits and Flaws

What follows are Merits and Flaws particularly suited to an elder chronicle and elder characters. Be sure to work with your Storyteller when you choose your Merits and Flaws, as some may interfere with the story or unbalance the game.

Merits and Flaws particularly suited for elders

Psychological — *Code of Honor, Compulsion, Dark Secret, Driving Goal, Higher Purpose, Intolerance, Nightmares, Phobia, Prey Exclusion, Short Fuse, Vengeance*

Mental — *Calm Heart, Deep Sleeper, Iron Will*

Aptitudes — *Illiterate, Jack of All Trades*

Supernatural — *Can't Cross Running Water, Cursed, Danger Sense, Dark Fate, Destiny, Faerie Affinity, Haunted, Light Sensitive, Luck, Magic Resistance, Magic Susceptibility, Medium, Occult Library, Repelled by Crosses, Repulsed by Garlic, Spirit Mentor, True Faith, Unbondable*

Kindred Ties — *Clan Enmity, Clan Friendship, Diabolic Sire, Enemy, Infamous Sire, Insane Sire, Notoriety, Pawn, Prestigious Sire, Reputation*

Physical — *Allergic (particularly to plastic, chemicals and other "modern" creations), Disfigured, Efficient Digestion, Misplaced Heart, Monstrous, Permanent Wound, Selective Digestion*

New Merits and Flaws

Holdings (1-5 Trait Merit)

You own a number of properties that have been in your possession for years. Most, if not all, have been modified to provide you with escape routes, shelter from the day, and protection. Examples include castles, museums, apartment complexes, cathedrals or even a series of underground caverns. For each point taken, you have two properties.

Enlightened (1-7 Trait Merit)

You have taken the first steps on the steep and thorny path of Golconda. While achievement of this state is a long way off, you understand the proper approach and spend much time in pursuit of this goal. A one-Trait Merit would mean that you know what the word means, and perhaps you are a beginner. Seven Traits would indicate that you have spent the better part of your existence in pursuit of Golconda, and that you are knowledgeable enough to teach your brethren the first lessons.

Laws of Elysium

Prestation Gifts (2-6 Trait Merit)

One or more Kindred owe you a boon. You granted them some form of assistance in the past (whether a hundred years ago, or just last week), but now they owe you. This will grant you an edge in dealing with them. Should you need aid, you can call the favors due, but you won't want to let these go lightly. Players should work with their Storytellers regarding the number of points in this Merit, and the circumstances of how these boons came to be. Factors in determining this should include the number and magnitude of the debts owed, and the positions of the Kindred who owe them.

Loyal Childe (3 Trait Merit)

Your childe's loyalty goes beyond the Blood Bond, borne of genuine admiration and affection. She would do almost anything to help you. Because her loyalty is so true, you can trust her like no other Kindred. Rest assured that she would give no rest to any who harmed you, and you would feel her loss as much as a stake through your own heart.

Paramour (3-5 Trait Merit)

You have had a long-term relationship (75-year minimum) with another Kindred. While you may have had disagreements over the years, you are generally loyal to each other. You both know a great deal about each other, and keep few secrets from one another. You have come to each other's aid several times, and the thought of losing him/her is something you would rather not consider. The cost of this Merit determines your lover's power and position in vampire society (three for an ancilla, four for an elder of equal stature, and five for a more powerful elder).

Poverty (1 Trait Flaw)

You are poor for an elder vampire. Maybe you just never saved anything over the years, maybe you lost your wealth in some catastrophe and have never recovered, or maybe you've given it away to whatever causes you patronize. You may not acquire any cash or other material wealth from your Influences.

Jilted Paramour (1-3 Trait Flaw)

You had a long-term affair (minimum of 50 years) with another Kindred. While the relationship was a pleasant diversion while it lasted, you eventually grew weary of your paramour and broke things off. Unfortunately, your paramour did not take this well and developed a strong resentment toward you. Or perhaps you were the jilted one, tossed aside like an unwanted doll by a bored child. You both know many of each other's secrets, and this has helped to keep things in a stalemate for now, but your ex- may interfere in your future affairs at a crucial time. The cost of this Flaw depends on the relative power and position of your ex-lover in Kindred society — one Trait for an ancilla, two for an elder of equal standing to you, and three for someone of higher standing.

Vainglorious (1-3 Trait Flaw)

You are the best, most beautiful, wisest, noblest, etc. Kindred that you know of, and you want to make sure that everyone knows it. You know that you deserve any praise you receive, since it is obvious the speaker recognizes quality when he sees it. You are especially fond of those who realize their lesser standing in comparison to your obvious superiority, and you tend to view those who speak well of you as more deserving and intelligent than most. Because of your arrogance, you must bid one to three Traits more in a Social Challenge to resist attempts to manipulate you through flattery. The modifier is determined by the rating in this Flaw.

Death Wish (1-5 Trait Flaw)

You have an unconscious wish for Final Death. The endless politicking and nightly hunts, the pain of centuries of living, your own immense knowledge and memory — all have taken their toll on you. While you would never deliberately harm yourself, you do tend to walk into dangerous situations and hinder yourself at the most awkward times. At any time during a session, the Storyteller may ask you to retest a challenge, with the less successful check being the actual result of your challenge. She may do this the number of times equal to the number of Traits you have in this Flaw.

Prestation Debt (1-5 Trait Flaw)

You currently owe a boon to one or more Kindred. You may have incurred this debt during the past, or just last week, but it's still outstanding to the Kindred in question. As such, she has gained some Status over you, which puts you at some disadvantage when dealing with her. At some point, she will call for the payment, and it could be a relatively minor service or something very uncomfortable for you.

The number of Traits invested in this Flaw must be determined between player and Storyteller. The number of debts, their magnitude and to whom they are owed determine the rating of this Flaw. The exact nature of how and to whom these debts were incurred should be worked out before play.

Bastard Childe (2 Trait Flaw)

You have sired one or more childer without permission from the local prince or the Justicar. By Kindred law, you and your childe could be Blood Hunted if your secret is discovered. This Flaw is cumulative, and must be taken once per bastard sired.

Vengeful Childe (2 Trait Flaw)

You have sired a childe who has grown to despise you. She actively hinders your dealings with other Kindred and works to your detriment.

You believe that your childe would commit diablerie on you given half a chance, and you're probably right.

Secret Diablerist (2 Trait Flaw)

You have committed diablerie at least once to achieve your current power, but so far no one knows your secret. Should your secret be learned, the other elders might well shun you, refuse you aid or turn against you, perhaps even calling the Blood Hunt. Do your utmost to keep this information secret. If your secret ever becomes known, you receive a three-Trait penalty on any Social Challenge with the elder who knows.

Recently Arisen (3 Trait Flaw)

You have been in torpor until recently. The world has left you behind in the rush of progress, and everything seems to have changed immensely while you slept. You experience culture shock on a nightly basis, and you have great difficulty making your way around this strange new society. Thankfully, Kindred society has not changed too much; mortal society is pure gibberish to you. You receive a two-Trait penalty when attempting to understand modern technology or society, and on social interactions with everyone but elder Kindred.

Matricide/Patricide (4 Trait Flaw)

You diablerized your own sire, one of the foulest crimes a vampire can commit. If ever this is discovered, you will almost certainly be left out for the sun. You've become an easy target for blackmail and must always be alert to any sign of other Kindred sniffing about for information regarding your sire's unusual "disappearance."

Known Diablerist (5 Trait Flaw)

You have committed diablerie at least once to achieve your power. Maybe it was during a Blood Hunt; maybe you simply got tired of waiting. While not every elder Kindred knows this, there are a few of note who do know, and you're sure they are spreading the word back through the ranks. At the very least, you would be shunned. At worst, you could be subject to the Blood Hunt, in spite of your status. Certain elders will probably use the information to blackmail you. You receive a three-Trait penalty on any Social Challenge with an elder who knows your secret.

Trait Maximums

As monstrous in power as elder characters may grow, even they have their limits. See **Laws of the Night** for the Trait maximums of each generation.

Character Creation

Age of Consideration

If you've been playing a vampire of elder years in your chronicle, maybe your interest got squicked while you were reading this, and you suddenly wanted to jump in on the elder game as well. After all, your character's old enough, and there are a lot of nifty things you'd love to acquire, not to mention getting the chance to kick a little vampiric tail. There's a certain Nosferatu character who's been getting too big for his britches in your opinion, and you could easily wipe the sewers with him — if you were an elder.

Before you start planning too much, stop and think. If you've been playing this character for some time, a number of people are going to be wondering why you've hidden your power and pretended to be so small all this time. Be assured that you'll be taken for something unpleasant (Infernalist, diablerist, Antediluvian pawn) if you suddenly "bulk up." And your powerful presence will certainly turn the game on its ear, and probably not for the better.

Talk it over with your Storyteller and listen to her concerns. If she agrees, work with her to create a plausible in-game reason why you've suddenly been elevated. Your new elder may get moved offstage to avoid unbalancing the game, but she might still be part of the action, if only in an advisory capacity. If the Storyteller decides not to bring an elder in, abide by her decision, and understand that it's for the good of the game.

Golconda

Few vampires are certain what Golconda means, how it can be achieved, or who can show them the way. Most consider it to be a dream, a fairy tale made up long ago by some poor benighted vampire who was moaning about the loss of his "human" side. The Sabbat actively denounce it as a lie perpetrated by the elders of the Camarilla, while most Camarilla elders dismiss it as the ravings of some forgotten lunatic. Behind the whispers and sneers, though, huddles a secret cabal (larger than some might think) that actively works to understand the mystery and hopefully achieve it. The mysterious Inconnu are all rumored to either be seeking Golconda or have already found it.

Golconda is said to be a mystical state of being in which the Beast and the Man no longer war with each other. The vampire has come to accept and master his Beast as a part of his soul no different than the

Man, and both are considered halves of the whole. Some claim that it grants a portion of one's humanity back, while others believe that it allows a vampire to live without the all-consuming need for blood.

A number of elder vampires take up the search when they grow weary of the machinations of their peers and of the endless nightly games. They seek out teachers wherever they may be found, perhaps one of the Salubri, or a teacher may come to them if they prove sufficiently ready for the task. What comprises the task is another matter. Some believe that one must give up feeding on mortals altogether, abandon the Jyhad, live one's unlife as an aescetic. What is known is that the culmination of the years of work is known as the Suspire, in which a vampire literally descends into the depths of her own soul for her "long dark night." Not everyone survives this final test, and not everyone who survives necessarily finds what they seek. Some may survive, but without achieving Golconda, making these the most embittered souls against the idea.

Storytellers wishing to add the search for Golconda into their chronicles should be prepared for a long haul. This is not a something to be dashed off in a month or even a year. A vampire can search for literally centuries for a few clues that lead to a teacher, and that is no guarantee that the teacher will accept her. A storyteller considering a Golconda chronicle needs to sit down and consider the framework of the story — what will be necessary for the seeker to find a teacher, what will it take for the teacher to accept the seeker, what will the seeker need to consider in her quest? How will this fit in with (or not) with your current plot and storylines? Will your elder's choice to give up the Jyhad send the current game into a tailspin? Plan out the necessary goals carefully, and know when to prod encouragingly and when to back off.

Likewise, a player needs to be made aware that for her character to begin seeking Golconda will be a most exacting goal to play over time, and that she can't just quit midstream because things aren't progressing as fast as she thinks they should be, or that by giving up drinking from mortals she should automatically be catapulted to her goal. A visit from an Inconnu or other seeker describing the rigors necessary to the character may be helpful to make the elder (and player) understand exactly what she is jumping into.

A search for Golconda need not necessarily move the character completely offstage. Golconda is denounced as a lie or fantasy by many, and other characters may see it as their duty to force the character to renounce her quest, which might create some intense roleplaying dynamics between the seeker and her former compatriots. Perhaps the seeker, in hunting for clues to finding a teacher, unearths a few other things, such as some interesting artifact, an embarrassing clan secret or an enemy she had long thought dead.

Gehenna Cults

The Camarilla officially decries Gehenna as a paranoid fallacy of the Sabbat, seeing the tales of the bloodthirsty Antediluvians as stories told to keep the unruly ones in line. *Officially*, Gehenna is seen as a myth by the elders and their ardent supporters. Behind closed doors, however, the whispers rise, and often the most staunch upholders of Blood Bonds and Traditions meet to discuss their secret fears. These are the most secret of the secret societies, for the exposure of one member places all in the gravest danger. The Inner Circle is not rumored to deal kindly with those Gehennists found.

These "Gehenna cults" are considered one of the last great thrills for many elders. There is something exhilarating in the danger of holding a carefully coded conversation at Elysium, powerful in seeking to defer the destruction of the world, and (dare it be said?) quite naughty in belonging to such a society. Membership in a cult, however exciting it might be, is a risky game, asking much of its members for a task that might in the end be all for nothing.

Some cults are social clubs with a secret Gehenna agenda known only to the "inner circle," while others array themselves in all manner of occultish trappings like Freemasons. Some have gone completely underground, approaching only those they believe to be completely sympathetic to their cause and only after extensive research to assure themselves of such. Most are small, a few having members that have met only through correspondence.

How these groups intend to bring about their ultimate goal varies according to the mission of the group. One searches for the "last daughter of Eve," said to be the herald of Gehenna according to *The Book of Nod*. Another searches for the last pieces of *The Book of Nod*, hoping that in a missing fragment will be the answer they seek. Other believe that they must show the Antediluvians they have been doing the work of good vampires, and seek to stamp out anarchs and humanists.

A few examples of Gehenna cults are given in **Elysium: The Elder Wars**. However, feel free to start your own for your chronicle which suits your purposes. After all, who's to say that those poor fools know the truth?

Clans and Paths

Elder Descriptions

While different circumstances wreak different changes upon each vampire, there are certain constants that can be seen in elders of the various clans.

The Camarilla

For the Camarilla, the endless nights bring the great game of intrigue and politics. The Camarilla's upper structure is supported largely by the elders — it is elders who form the Inner Circle, and elders who serve as the feared Justicars. They enjoy pride of place as the movers and shakers of Kindred society, and do not hesitate to use their accumulated power to remind the "youngsters" of this. However, they have used such power to the detriment of the Camarilla as a whole, clinging to their positions long past their usefulness and killing the best and brightest they fear as threats.

As elders age, the thoughts of Golconda often become more and more frequent. Those who have managed to cling to their Humanity begin to consider the path in earnest, particularly when they find the ravages of age (callousness, paranoia, cannibalism) creeping upon them. Few, however, have the spiritual mettle to take more than a step or two. Those who choose the path often secretly follow and study it until they feel they are far enough along that they can make a full-time effort of it. Only the secure (in respect to faith and society) dare to step away.

Brujah

Brujah elders are often deep into the politics of cities and Kindred — and are very good at them. They wield great influence in the clan, not necessarily because the young ones respect them (indeed, most will watch the elders like hawks for signs of "selling out"), but because the young ones know that their elders hold power and are not afraid to use it when necessary. Time has tempered these elders (although they are still prone to frenzy), and most have left behind the Iconoclast days of their youth, but they have not given up their ideals of freedom and justice. They have simply moved into more "genteel" forums.

Gangrel

Like the Lupines they emulate, Gangrel elders are prized and respected as keepers of wisdom and warriors without peer — when they can be found. Some become solitaries, maintaining private havens in the wild which they defend from any incursion, while others drift into city living and politics. Many have become extremely bestial from frenzies over the years, often sporting such touches as tufted ears, tails, extreme hairiness or animal eyes. Some of these elders can no longer be seen in human society unless they use a Discipline such as *Mask of 1000 Faces*.

Malkavians

Kooks who reach elder age are some of the most disturbing (and disturbed) Kindred one is likely to meet. When they decide to pull out their bags of tricks, chances are the tricks will be intricate and lethal. Their Derangements intensify over time, but they are hardly erratic or childish. Crazy doesn't mean inefficient, and those who have chosen to play the elders' games do so with the skill of consummate chess-players.

Clans and Paths

Nosferatu

Clannish and solitary, most Nosferatu elders are in a position to sit in the middle of the spider's web and watch the youngsters scurry. Many do, collecting the lore of centuries from networks of runners, and they boast some of the most impressive libraries of Kindred lore. Those who choose to play the political games do so with as much at their commands as they can muster.

Toreador

No clan is as aware of the passage of time and temporality as the Toreador. For the elders, watching the parade of fashion and art endlessly pass before them eventually drags many into ennui. Some watch the rise of artistic movements with a practiced eye, judging those they deem worthy of support or ridicule. Toreador are some of the most likely to fall into degeneracy as they age, "requiring" more extreme pleasures to excite their senses.

Those Artistes who have managed to pursue their art even after so many years often reach a technical brilliance that is almost inconceivable to the human mind. As they age, however, they may find themselves growing distant from the "human" element of their work, resulting in art that fulfills the demands of technique, but which becomes cold and impersonal to its viewers.

Tremere

Most of the Tremere's elders occupy the higher echelons of the pyramid of power, reaching their positions through a combination of skill, politicking and sheer tenacity. These are considered the leaders and tradition-bearers, teachers and masters, and in the hierarchical arrangement of this former wizards' cabal, age demands (and receives) respect. They watch their younger clansmen with trepidation, walking a fine line between reward and punishment. By virtue of the clan's structure, elders may easily deny potentially "dangerous" neonates and ancillae of rank with little question from their superiors and peers.

Ventrue

Repositories of Kindred tradition, many elder Ventrue can be found in the thick of city politics as princes or primogen. The eldest among them almost always have such experience under their belts. Never known for "daring" ways, even as neonates and ancillae, elder Ventrue can be among the most hidebound, and they will resist change in any form simply because it upsets their careful routines.

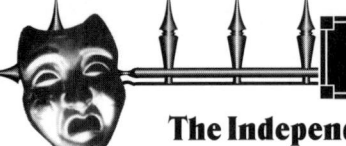

Laws of Elysium

The Independents

Elders of the independent clans and bloodlines usually maintain the greatest status among their own. At such age and power, some feel they may venture out among the ruck and run of Kindred society without too much curiosity regarding their business. The idly curious can be sent packing, while the elders of the established clans may be receptive to deal-making with a surprising ally.

Few elders of the independents ever reach their age through charm. Indeed, for some of these, merely reaching the age of discretion is an accomplishment in and of itself.

Assamite

These are among the most feared of vampirekind, and with good reason. All are experienced assassins with numerous kills to their records, some more than others. They are considered the "priesthood," the teachers of the neonates and the guides of the ancillae. Eldership is not usually based on age alone; appointment to the *silsila* can be made by the clan leaders in recognition of outstanding service and dedication to the clan's ideals.

Daughters of Cacophony

There are no known Daughters below the seventh generation. However, these *rara avis* are viewed with trepidation, if not fear, by many, including elders. Their gifts of song, channeled through *Melpominee*, are little known and even less understood, and rumors of elder Daughters combining their voices into a destructive symphony is enough to set any Elysium buzzing.

Followers of Set

Elder Setites often sit in the center of empires of corruption carefully built over centuries of work. Often they use younger Setites to build their works, even as the ancillae believe that they are forwarding their own ventures. Their blood is extremely addictive; it is unknown how many scramble and scheme to get their "fix," but many elder Setites gloat over the number of peers who have fallen to such needs.

Giovanni

Elder Giovanni rule the clan with iron fists, often powerful and completely ruthless. These become the legendary dons of Mafia families, unsinkable patriarchs and iron-willed matriarchs who control their networks of spies and thugs with devastating efficiency.

Very little happens in the rank and file without their knowledge or approval. As necromancers, they have lived long enough to acquire a frightening number of wraithly alliances and enemies.

Ravnos

Elder Ravnos often head fairly large *kumpania*, whether physically or spiritually. Even if they have chosen to wander as solitaries, the *kumpania* welcomes them back whenever they return. Gypsies prize their elders as repositories of wisdom and lore, and such is drilled into the heads of the youngsters (whether human or vampire) at an early age. Often, elder Ravnos have particular tricks and cons that they have honed to consummate skill from years of practice.

Salubri

Rare in the extreme, those Salubri who have reached elder age have often done so with the help of allies and through their own wits. A Salubri who has not reached Golconda by this time is quite unusual. Those who have are expected to create childer and extinguish themselves through ritual diablerie. They may be sheltered at a prince's court as advisors or teachers of Golconda, but they are always aware that at any moment they may need to flee from a Tremere with "righteousness" on his mind.

Samedi

Solitary and often bitter, Samedi elders find quiet havens and prefer to be left entirely alone. If one can be drawn out of his solitude, he is often quite knowledgeable about decay and the passing of time. Some choose tombs which they study over the course of years, observing nightly changes of decay in the inhabitants.

The Sabbat

In the violence of Sabbat society, elder status is a plum prize indeed, particularly since it means one survived long enough to achieve it. Sabbat elders are looked to as examples of the best, and they need to prove it every single night; there are always youngsters with delusions of grandeur who need to be reminded of their place. Resting on one's laurels is not advised, and often an elder doesn't have the time. More often than not, Sabbat elders are serving in high-ranking positions such as paladins and bishops, and are called on to teach the next generation of fighters. Among the packs, an elder who has managed to hold her own for so long will likely be a battle-scarred pack leader or an experienced priest.

Sabbat elders are viewed with trepidation and awe by their younger brethren. No one wants an elder's eye turned on her, and even those who receive favorable attention are never wholly comfortable in the presence of the elder until much time and experience has shown them otherwise. It was, after all, the elders and their loathsome deeds that started the Anarch Revolt.

Lasombra

Admission to the prestigious ranks of *Les Amies Noir* is considered the hallmark of "eldership" for the Lasombra. Great privilege and great responsibility mark one's time as an elder. Failure is not tolerated, so one may be certain that a Lasombra elder is among the best of her kind. A great number serve in the upper ranks of the Sabbat as bishops and other leaders; indeed, it is a Lasombra elder who rules Mexico City. Often chief in their mind is the embarrassing presence of the *antitribu*, and they will pursue any rumors of such to exhaustion.

Tzimisce

Many Tzimisce of advanced age no longer look remotely human, having practiced *Vicissitude* on themselves to reflect their increasingly alien state of mind. Scorning humans as juicebags and annoyances, they see no reason to look like them either. They often lord over what land they still own as their own, dreaming of days in the Carpathians and mixing old-fashioned ideals of manners, kingship and custom with utterly inhuman desires and whims. The cruelty of elder Tzimisce is legendary among the youth, who quickly learn to keep a civil tongue in their heads before it is removed for them. Many are highly superstitious beyond their clan weakness of sleeping in native soil.

Caitiff

The average Caitiff is considered at a ripe old age if she survives to become an ancilla. Most rarely achieve elder status, primarily because they are driven from cities and hunted to the ground. Those who have reached the age of consideration are often loners, preferring their own company to that of their unkind brethren. A few manage to gather broods around them, usually of their own childer and grandchilder. On occasion, they go insane from the lack of Kindred company, and either end their existences or turn to preying on the society that cast them out in the first place.

Clans and Paths

New Clans

The following clans are included here, since the majority of their ranks tend to be those of elder age. It is unlikely that many below ancilla rank have heard much of substance about them beyond stories of their sires.

Gargoyles

Created in the Dark Ages to serve the Tremere as terrifying warriors and servants, the first Gargoyles were molded from the raw matter of captured vampires steeped in foul alchemical ichors. Using strange rituals, the Tremere conjured puissant guardians who provide strong defense and unyielding loyalty to the various chantries. Upon the change, Gargoyles lose all memory of their previous lives, and suffer agonizing physical and spiritual changes. Magically bound to service, Gargoyles exist only to fight the enemies of their masters.

Some Gargoyles break free of their conditioning, seeking to revolt against their Tremere masters. Still, the ties of their generative magic are strong, and few can hope to escape slavery. In modern years, the Tremere carefully separate Gargoyles, assigning only one or two to any given location, so as to quash any revolt. The individual Gargoyle remains a sad and lonely figure, enthralled in servitude, lacking any but the faintest memories of a former life, and driven to great rage and frustration.

Clan Disciplines: *Fortitude, Potence, Visceratika*

Advantage: Gargoyles are all created through a magical ritual, which imbues them with unnatural resilience. All Gargoyles gain one additional Health Level — treat this as an extra "Healthy" level on the wound levels chart.

Disadvantage: Gargoyles suffer from a rocklike, inhuman appearance, sometimes studded with strange pebbly growths. They quite literally resemble something that crawled down from the tower of a Gothic cathedral, complete with wings, horns, talons and tails that continue to grow as they age. Thus, a Gargoyle automatically fails any Social Challenge not related to intimidation when its normal form is visible. Gargoyle players should wear enough makeup to make their inhuman appearance obvious, or should at least adopt baggy clothing and accesories that could reasonably conceal the Gargoyle form.

Furthermore, as a magically created servitor race, gargoyles are automatically two Traits down on any attempt to resist *Dominate* or other forms of supernatural mind control.

Dark Ages Gargoyles

Clan Disciplines: *Flight, Fortitude, Potence*

Advantage: Gargoyles of the Dark Ages gain an additional Health Level, just like their modern counterparts.

Disadvantage: Gargoyles in the Dark Ages suffer from the same hindrances as their successors.

Note: The Discipline of *Visceratika* actually consists of several powers that were bestowed upon Gargoyles through the use of Thaumaturgical rituals; by the modern age, the typical Gargoyle has internalized those powers. In the Dark Ages, the Discipline of *Visceratika* is not available to Gargoyles, but the individual powers of the Discipline may be studied as Thaumaturgy rituals of the same difficulty (i.e. a Basic *Visceratika* power can be learned as a Basic ritual). These rituals, which only function on a Gargoyle, typically require the expenditure of a Mental Trait by the caster and last for the duration of the session.

Dark Ages Gargoyles gain the ability to fly instead of studying *Visceratika*; they spend experience points as if buying the *Visceratika* Discipline, but each level purchased allows the Gargoyle to fly at a speed of 5 mph. Thus, a Gargoyle with four levels of *Flight* can fly at a speed of 20 mph. Flight should be represented with a special card or hand signal, prearranged with a Narrator or Storyteller.

Lasombra *Antitribu*

These renegade Kindred have nearly been hunted to extinction by their Sabbat brethren. Many are relics of the Middle Ages who refused to join with the Sabbat after the fall of their Antediluvian founder. While similar in many aspects to their Sabbat counterparts, Lasombra *antitribu* are cunning and ruthless survivors who will stop at nothing to ensure their continued existence. Be it piracy on the high seas or controlling the stock market, they are masters of adapting to a situation to serve their needs. A few are members of the Camarilla, but most are independents who serve their own interests.

Disciplines: *Dominate, Obtenebration, Potence*

Advantage: Lasombra *antitribu* are master manipulators and businessmen. Because of this, they automatically gain one additional *Bureaucracy* or *Finance* Influence Trait.

Clans and Paths

Disadvantage: In addition to the standard Lasombra disadvantage regarding mirrors, Lasombra *antitribu* are distrusted within the Camarilla, and have the permanent Negative Trait of *Untrustworthy* as a result. In addition, the Lasombra *antitribu*, be they Camarilla or independent, are constantly hunted without remorse by Lasombra of the Sabbat.

Old Clan Tzimisce

Ancient beyond most Kindred standards, those Tzimisce that never embraced the *Vicissitude* Discipline are known as the "Old Clan." While similar to their modern Sabbat counterparts in their inhuman natures and macabre tastes, they carry a seething hatred for their *Vicissitude*-using childer, whom they consider to be traitors of their blood. Most of these rare vampires still maintain large estates and castles that they have lorded over for centuries. Nearly all are unliving antiquities, often dressing and speaking in fashions outdated for centuries. The Old Clan Tzimisce are for the most part solitary, vicious independents who do not acknowledge the sovereignty of either the Camarilla or the Sabbat. They rarely receive visitors to their domains, but those who have gained admittance speak in awe of the storehouses of knowledge to be found.

Disciplines: *Animalism, Auspex, Dominate*

Advantage: Old Clan Tzimisce show innate magical aptitude, such that if taught *Thaumaturgy* they are not required to pay the one extra experience point normally required for all out-of-clan Disciplines.

Disadvantage: Something deep inside the Old Clan craves stability and permanence. The Fiends share a special connection to the land they claimed as their own in life. When they slumber, these ancient Kindred must surround themselves with at least two handfuls of earth from a land important to them in life. Failure to do so results in a fitful day's rest, and no Willpower or Attributes Traits are regained from the sleep.

Beast/Path Traits

A character not on one of the Paths of Enlightenment is automatically considered to be on the Path of Humanity. Unlike Beast Traits, Path Traits have an undisputed hierarchy of sins that if broken demand an automatic Path Trait check. See **Laws of the Night** (pp. 40-44) for rules on Paths.

Laws of Elysium

Hierarchy of Sins

The Hierarchies of Sins were not included in **LotN**, nor was the Path of Humanity. They are therefore printed here for the use of your troupe.

Path of Caine

Failing to pursue evidence concerning Caine when it could cost you your unlife.

Failing to spend at least 10 minutes in meditation every night.

Acting against the Sabbat.

Being disrespectful to your elders.

Failing to participate in a War Party.

Refusing to attempt to destroy or convert Camarilla vampires.

Considering humans to be of any more value than as food sources.

Feeling sorry for killing a human.

Not killing a mortal when there is need to do so.

Relying on human allies or friends.

Path of Cathari

Refusing to sire new vampires.

Failing to pursue a new form of pleasure.

Failing to ride the wave of frenzy.

Avoiding injury to others at the cost of your own pleasure.

Refusing to murder humans when it would be in your best interest.

Refusing to commit cruel acts that are in your best interest.

Failing to brag about yourself if it is a good opportunity.

Turning down a chance at material gain.

Acting altruistically.

Restraining yourself unnecessarily.

Path of Death and the Soul

Failing to kill for the sake of knowledge.

Showing fear of Final Death.

Acting in an emotional manner.

Riding the wave during frenzy.

Showing any sign of the animal or the human in you.

Failing to study death when the opportunity affords itself.

Showing no interest in death, or an aversion to it.

Clans and Paths

Displaying overt compassion.

Needlessly preventing death.

Allowing your emotion to override your logic.

Path of Harmony

Failing to spend at least 10 minutes per night communing alone with nature.

Killing an animal for any reason other than survival.

Failing to hunt and drink blood when needed.

Acting in an overly cruel manner.

Refusing to ride the wave as long as it is not detrimental to your own survival.

Killing a mortal for any reason other than survival.

Failing to provide safety for your loved ones and comrades.

Allowing yourself to act too human or too bestial (Storyteller's discretion).

Feeling guilty about doing something you needed to do.

Refusing to kill when it is important to your survival.

Path of Honorable Accord

Failing to act in accordance with the Sabbat in any matter.

Failing to show hospitality to other Sabbat.

Failing to observe an *Ignoblis Ritus* of your pack.

Failing to observe an *Auctoritas Ritus* of the Sabbat.

Acting against your leader; failing to protect fellow Sabbat.

Placing personal welfare over that of the entire sect.

Failing to honor an agreement.

Showing cowardice.

Showing overt disrespect for the sect.

Breaking your word.

Path of Humanity

Wanton destruction.

Not resisting frenzy.

Going against one's Nature.

Killing a mortal.

Torturing someone.

Embracing a mortal out of spite.

Betraying your sect, clan, etc. to the enemy.

Bringing about the unlawful destruction of a Kindred in the same sect, clan, etc.

Committing diablerie.

Dealing with the infernal.

Path of Power and the Inner Voice

Spending fewer than 10 minutes per night in silent meditation.

Failing to use whatever means necessary to achieve greater power.

Accepting defeat.

Helping others when it is not to your advantage.

Failing to respect others who possess greater power and wisdom.

Treating underlings poorly.

Backing down when you know you are right.

Turning down a chance for increased wealth or power.

Losing face in a crowd.

Accepting someone who is equally or less capable than yourself as your superior.

Clan-Specific Paths

The following paths are clan-specific, and almost never seen among vampires not of the clan. They can be taught to other clans only through in-play interaction, and may never be taken by a character outside of the specific clan at character creation. Like clan-specific Disciplines, the Paths are usually kept as tight secrets among the clan members; teaching them to outsiders may be considered a betrayal.

Assamite

Path of Blood

Outsiders often interpret the Assamite belief in the Path of Blood as a simple desire for increased power through diablerie. The truth is much more complex, embedded in the teachings of Haqim (the Assamite founder) which form the central motivation for the clan.

The Path of Blood teaches that it will lead to the downfall of the Camarilla, turning their own strength against them. This will lead to the fulfillment of the Assamites' revenge for their sufferings, as well as carrying out Haqim's sacred task of ridding the world of the Kindred.

Clans and Paths

The second (and more mystical teaching) is that the Path of Blood ascends the peak of Alamut, and the Assamite who climbs the Path of Blood to the summit shall become One. This esoteric concept involves achieving a kind of enlightenment directly comparable to the Camarilla idea of Golconda. Only by reaching the summit may an Assamite become One.

In many ways, this teaching is very similar to the Sabbat's Path of Caine, which the Assamites are often credited with developing. The Camarilla are allowed to carry on believing that the Assamites follow the Path of Caine, since this is in the interests of the Great Disguise and prevents outsiders from learning their true goal: the destruction of all Caine's progeny.

Path of Blood Hierarchy of Sins:

Failing to pursue an opportunity to obtain Kindred blood of a higher generation than your own, though it may cost your unlife.

Succumbing to frenzy.

Failing to pursue Kindred blood or knowledge of Caine or the Curse when there is moderate danger.

Being disrespectful to clan leaders.

Failing to execute an assassination contract yet surviving.

Failing to pursue blood or knowledge in the face of minor danger.

Not killing a non-Assamite vampire when there is need to do so.

Placing personal desires or ambition above other matters.

Failing to assist or avenge a clanmate.

Revealing clan information to outsiders.

Path Traits

Assamites on the Path of Blood may also choose from the Path Traits *Abelite*, *Self-Controlled* or *Scholar* as described in **Laws of the Night**. (pp. 41) under the Path of Caine.

• Avenger — You believe in clan loyalty above all else. If anyone attempts to stop you or a clanmate from assisting or avenging a fellow Assamite, you succumb to a bloody killing haze to accomplish your goal.

• Disrespect — Frenzy whenever you see a fellow Assamite treat a higher-ranking Assamite with disrespect of any sort. Assamites must treat all, even enemies, with the respect due to them. The idea of a clanmate lowering himself to the level of other inferior vampires disgusts you.

- **Failure** — Your clan has a reputation as the perfect killers. If you, or a fellow Assamite that you are aware of, fail in an assassination attempt, your self-esteem drops you into a frenzy-ridden depression of low morale.

- **Traitor** — If you are forced to reveal clan secrets to others, you succumb to frenzy. Treason is the worst crime an Assamite can commit. Frenzy if you become aware of an Assamite betraying the clan. Frenzy if you see a non-clanmate using powers or information that they could have only learned through an Assamite teaching (and betrayal).

Ravnos

Path of Paradox

The Path of Paradox teaches that all existence is fluid and malleable. Nothing is permanent or real. The universe is an ever-shifting vortex and all in it is composed of variable amounts of ethereal matter, called "*weig*."

Ravnos on this Path gradually learn their *raison d'àtre*: to destroy the blasphemous creation of the Antediluvians, that thing known as reality. They learn to harness their internal *weig* for the production of reality-altering effects. These effects are mere illusions at low levels of power, but as the Ravnos becomes more powerful, the "tricks" gradually increase in potency.

Ravnos also actively attempt to alter others' perceptions of reality. Their favorite methods for so doing are through trickery and theft. Such are surprisingly effective weapons.

Ultimately, however, the *weig* must be released into the vortex. Ravnos who are advanced students of this Path actively seek out items that retain weig — "magic" items, Lupine fetishes and the like — and destroy them. The most powerful followers of this Path hunt vampires with great amounts of *weig* — low generation, and the lower the better.

Path of Paradox Hierarchy of Sins

Refusing to commit diablerie upon an elder of another clan.

Refusing to lead a "locked" being into the light — or into destruction.

Showing any concern for mortals.

Failing to acquire items or knowledge that would affect Gehenna.

Failing to trick others when the opportunity arises.

Being caught altering another's reality via the select redistribution of possessions (known among the vulgar as stealing).

Refusing to release the *weig* of an empowered device.

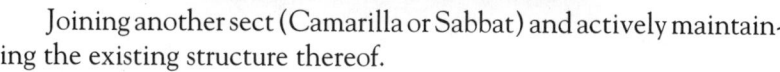

Clans and Paths

Joining another sect (Camarilla or Sabbat) and actively maintaining the existing structure thereof.

Actively hindering change.

Actively inducing boredom.

Path Traits

• Release — Frenzy whenever you are prevented from committing diablerie on an elder of another clan, or releasing the *weig* from any contained item. If someone else is getting in your way, remove him.

• Concern — Mortals are an unimaginative and boring lot that refuse to see the big picture. Vampires who dote on them infuriate you! Frenzy if you must watch Kindred pamper or care for these unenlightened dolts.

• Knowledge — Frenzy whenever someone directly prevents you from acquiring knowledge of Gehenna. If a Nosferatu dangles pages of *The Book of Nod* in front of your face and refuses to let you see it, you frenzy.

• Failure — Frenzy if you are caught trying to pull a heist of any sort, whether a simple riddle, trick, theft, etc. "Real" Ravnos can get away with anything if they want to. You screwed up — you *hate* that!

• Boredom — You hate being bored. Boredom means stagnation, means that *weig* is getting trapped. You'll frenzy just to shake things up. If you find yourself getting bored during the evening's session, you frenzy (this is only if your *character* is bored; player boredom is another matter entirely).

Setites

Path of Typhon

Certainly no Setites are more sinister than those who follow the shadowy Path of Typhon. Its tenets are anathema to all that most mortals, and many Kindred, hold dear. For the Typhonites, corruption, pain, lies and sin are things to be cherished and spread throughout existence. Misery is not a means to an end, but an end in and of itself.

Of all the Paths, the Path of Typhon is more like a religion than a philosophy. Its practitioners are rumored to worship various entities — perhaps personifications of various sins, perhaps something else — through blood libations and sacrifice. Through such worship, the Typhonites believe, mystic understanding may be gleaned.

In order to achieve enlightenment, the followers of this Path continually seek to spread war, plague, poverty, stagnation and fear through the world. Through the creation and study of such phenomena, the Typhonites hope to discover the truths about, and behind, earthly existence. As far as the followers of Typhon are concerned, everyone else is missing the point.

Path of Typhon Hierarchy of Sins

Attempting to maintain any sense of self-control, purity or worth.

Refusing to succumb to one's own weaknesses (this includes attempting to avoid frenzy).

Failing to destroy a vampire in Golconda.

Destroying a foe expediently and mercifully rather than "poetically."

Failing to undermine the current social order in favor of the Setites.

Failing to replace faith with cynicism and despair.

Failing to exploit another's weaknesses.

Allowing one's feelings for a mortal to override the need to corrupt said mortal.

Refusing to corrupt a vampire for the Setites.

Not attempting to awaken Set at the earliest opportunity.

Path Traits

• **Control** — You should have what you want. Should anyone decide to try to control your actions, you frenzy and make sure that she never tries it again.

• **Weakness** — The idea of someone fighting off his personal weakness infuriates you. Frenzy whenever you fail to get someone to give in to his weakness.

• **Purity** — The idea of those dolts that attempt to promote goodness and that vile concept of Golconda disgusts you like little else. When you are confronted with anyone holy or pure, you feel the overwhelming urge to destroy her. If prevented, you frenzy. If ever confronted by the Children of Osiris, a Salubri or anyone using the Disciplines of *Bardo* or *Obeah*, you frenzy on the spot.

• **Mortal Feelings** — If your feelings for a mortal conflict with your desire to corrupt her, the conflict within you drives you mad. The Beast takes control and you frenzy.

• **Knowledge of Set** — Frenzy whenever someone directly prevents you from acquiring knowledge of Set, such as a museum guard refusing to let you get closer to a scrap of papyrus on display.

Path of Ecstasy

Practitioners of this Path revel in luxury instead of degradation. They sate the Beast by glutting its appetite. Although akin to the Path of Typhon in some ways, Ecstatics reject the base cruelties of the Typhonites. Rather than celebrate misery, they glorify pleasure, reveling in the most decadent extremes of vampiric sensation. Members of this path often despise the Kindred of Clan Toreador, and take every opportunity to humiliate them.

Path of Ecstasy Hierarchy of Sins

Allowing someone innocent to survive.

Not wallowing in absolute luxury.

Allowing someone ugly to survive.

Allowing an infector of impurity (i.e., priest, nun, etc.) to live without good reason.

Rejecting wealth unnecessarily.

Not attempting to corrupt an innocent.

Not taking at least one drug regularly.

Restraining your natural impulses unnecessarily.

Failing to accept a gift.

Destroying something of beauty.

Path Traits

• **Innocence** — You always kill mortals that you feed upon. That's what they are here for, after all. If a victim happens to escape death at your hands during your feeding, you frenzy. You played with your food too much, and now it got away!

• **Luxury** — You love your luxurious lifestyle. The thought of losing it makes you want to destroy anyone who would take it from you. Frenzy if you happen to lose anything that is yours.

• **Corruption** — The drive to corrupt the innocent is like a drug to you. If you fail to corrupt a chosen target, your anger is without equal. If he cannot be corrupted, he must be destroyed. You will remove anyone that gets between you and your target.

• **Addiction** — You have become addicted to a foreign substance or drug. If you can't get your "fix" at least once per session, you frenzy.

• **Beauty** — Beauty is meant to be cherished. The sight of something beautiful being destroyed causes the Beast to rise within you, with a vengeance! You instantly frenzy and go looking for the despoiler. Barring him, you'll take anyone who gets in your way.

Path of the Warrior

This Path has grown in popularity in recent decades, with many young Setites attracted to its philosophies. Just as Set was once a hunter and warrior, so too are adherents of this Path. These Setites pride themselves upon their physical and martial prowess. Many who follow the Path of the Warrior are masochists and fanatics. They believe that the Beast is a creation of the mind, and that by training the body until it is stronger than the mind, the Beast can be controlled.

Path of the Warrior Hierarchy of Sins

Not subjecting yourself to the most painful tortures.

Failing any test set you, physical or mental.

Not developing your body to its fullest potential.

Spending Blood Points to heal your wounds the same night they are inflicted.

Not developing your Disciplines to their fullest potential.

Killing swiftly and mercifully.

Showing any sign of pain.

Not exercising every night.

Thinking too long before acting.

Refusing a Physical Challenge.

Path Traits

• Failure — The mind and body Set provided you are the most powerful things you have. Frenzy if you fail in a conflict regarding the power of your mind or proving your superior physical prowess.

• Mental or Physical Development — If you are unable to spend at least half an hour per night in meditation or developing your near-perfect immortal body, you are forced into a panic-driven frenzy.

• Discipline Development — If you are not able to successfully use at least one each of your different Disciplines on a foe per night, you frenzy out of shame at your own weakness.

• Pain — Pain is for the weak. Only inferior beings show pain. If you are caught showing any pain, you have failed Set. Knowing that you have failed Set causes you to frenzy.

• Refusal — Refusing a Physical Challenge dishonors Set. If you or any other Setite that you see backs down from a Physical Challenge, you frenzy due to the dishonor to your lord.

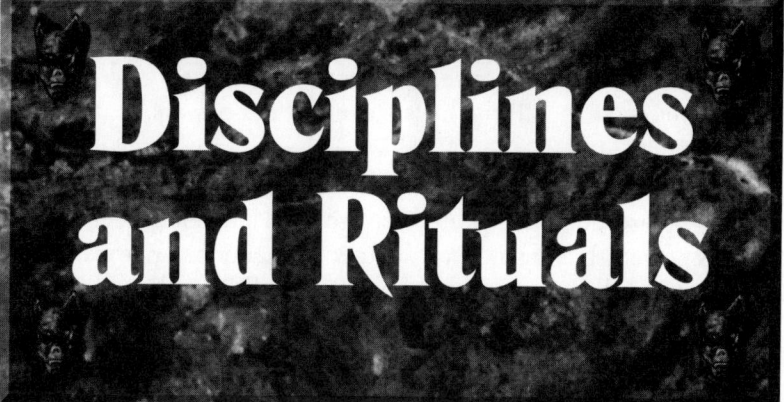

Disciplines

Even the youngest vampire is aware of the powers bestowed on her by virtue of her blood, and over time and through testing, she can create some remarkable and lethal effects. With such immense time to hone one's abilities, the powers of the elder vampires are terrifying and amazing to behold.

Characters of the ninth generation and higher may learn Advanced Disciplines, but they may not progress beyond them, forcing these Kindred to seek other ways to enhance their personal power. The same is not true for those of older vitae. Characters of the eighth generation and lower have access to the potent Master-level Disciplines. As with any Discipline the lower levels must be learned before moving on to the more advanced powers; before learning *Soul Scan*, for instance, a character must possess *Clairvoyance*, *Psychic Projection* and all the lower-level *Auspex* powers.

Master-level powers cost 12 experience points per clan Discipline and 13 points per out-of-clan. Characters that possess these frightening powers are uncommon at best. Storytellers should feel free to disallow powers that are too easily abused or that unbalance the game. In addition to the Master-level powers, the following Disciplines — *Melpominee, Mytherceria, Necromancy, Obeah, Quietus, Spiritus* and *Thanatosis* — have been given an additional Basic power for game balance. These powers are to be learned in order with those Basic powers listed in **Laws of the Night** (e.g., the *Quietus* power *Weakness* would be learned after *Silence of Death* and before *Poison Blade*). The *Thaumaturgy* Paths and Rituals listed in this supplement are available to characters of any generation.

Animalism

Master

Animal Succulence

While many Kindred find the blood of animals revolting and detest consuming their vitae, you are able to reap unique benefits from this type of feeding. *Animal Succulence* makes animal vitae particularly nourishing, and doubles the number of Blood Traits a vampire with this Discipline may obtain from any animal. This power is not in effect when a vampire feeds on humans.

Conquer the Beast

You now have achieved a certain mastery of the Beast within yourself. As such, you may enter and exit any frenzy at will. You may choose and control the type of frenzy you enter (see **Laws of the Night**, pp. 117-118) and your actions throughout. To enter frenzy, you must lose one Social Trait and one Willpower Trait. The frenzy ends whenever you so choose, or after 10 minutes have elapsed. A character in frenzy gains the following:

Rage Frenzy: *Ferocious* x 2 and *Tenacious*

Control Frenzy: *Ferocious* x 2 and *Tough*

Terror Frenzy: *Ferocious* x 2 and *Brutal*, plus immunity to *Presence*, *Dominate* and any other non-*Animalism* Social Challenge.

Disciplines and Rituals

Auspex

Master

Clairvoyance

You can see and hear events without the need for *Psychic Projection*. To use this Discipline, you must win a Static Mental Challenge against a variable difficulty (see chart). The difficulty of the challenge is based on your familiarity with the place you seek to view (e.g., *Clairvoyantly* viewing your own haven would be a Static Challenge against a difficulty of four Traits, while viewing your sire's castle in Transylvania that you have only seen in a painting is a nearly impossible task). You may also use all other *Auspex* Disciplines while using *Clairvoyance*.

Place as familiar as one's haven	4
Visited there three or four times	8
Visited once	12
Described in detail	18
Never been there but have seen a photograph	25

Soul Scan

You can discover the "location" of anyone you know, wherever the target may be. This power requires the assistance of a Narrator. You must win a Static Mental Challenge against the target's Mental Traits to enact this Discipline. The Narrator simply notes the time of the *Soul Scan* and then finds the target, asking her where she was at that time and informing you. Other Disciplines (as appropriate) can be used after locating the target. This power locates the mind of the individual sought. If the individual sought is currently using powers such as *Psychic Projection* or *Possession*, the result of *Soul Scan* will be to find where her conscious mind currently is.

Bardo

Master

Bring Forth the Dawn

With this power you may force another Kindred to succumb to the Daysleep by winning a Social Challenge against him. The victim will sleep one hour for every Beast Trait he has. This power can also affect multiple targets (Mob Rule applies). The target can only be aroused by circumstances which would directly bring about his destruction (Storyteller's discretion). The target may, if he chooses, spend Willpower to remain awake, at a rate of one Trait per hour.

Celerity

Master

Quickness

You disappear, in an incredible burst of speed. Your synchronicity between mind and body has reached such a level of perfection that most Kindred deem the speed in which you move unfathomable. You may make four extra challenges when employing *Quickness*. Otherwise this power is identical to *Swiftness*, including cost. If used to cut travel time, the time is reduced to 1/16.

Velocity

Vampires with this power are often mistaken for having the powers of teleportation. You move faster than most conscious minds can think. You may make five extra challenges when employing *Velocity*. Otherwise this power is identical to *Swiftness*, including cost. If used to cut travel time, the time is reduced to 1/32.

Chimerstry

Basic (Level 2)

Fata Morgana

You can create an illusion that is visible to one person. However, the illusion you create may affect as many senses as you wish, including sight, sound, touch and even smell and taste. While the created illusion is not real and cannot cause physical harm, it can be used to trick or deceive others after a successful Social Challenge. The illusion lasts for as long as you want it to, until you leave the vicinity, or until your opponent succeeds in a Social Challenge.

Master

Pseudo Blindness

Your ability to perceive reality has reached a heightened state well beyond that of other Kindred. Where once you were as easily duped as any other, you now no longer fall prey to simple mind tricks. You are no longer affected by *Obfuscate* or *Chimerstry* powers below Advanced, unless your adversary is of a lower generation than yourself. Once acquired, this power is in effect at all times.

Disciplines and Rituals

Mass Reality

The illusions you now create have become so potent that you can cause whole groups of people to experience *Horrid Reality*. All of your opponents see the same illusion and believe it to be real. You must win a Mental Challenge against each target in turn for this power to be successful.

Dementation

Master

Kindred Spirits

You can manipulate another's mind and force the victim to become identical to you in many respects. The target's Nature and Demeanor temporarily change to match your own. In addition, the victim acquires any Derangements and all Beast/Path Traits you possess. This power does not give you any direct control over the victim, but while under its effects, she is forced to act in ways that she normally would not. You must make physical contact (which may result in a Physical Challenge) and succeed in a Mental Challenge for this power to take effect. The duration of this power is one hour. At Narrator discretion, an extended test can grant an additional hour of effect for each success earned.

Mind of a Killer

This power allows you to alter the mind of your target, making her a cold-blooded killer. The first person to offend the target in any way (including a loved one or an opponent of considerably more power) becomes her chosen victim. The target will then do everything in her power to kill her chosen victim, using whatever means it takes. So strong is the target's hatred that when in the presence of her victim, she must win a Static Mental Challenge every 10 minutes or she will frenzy and attack the target. Once the target has completed her task, the effect ends and the target is left to agonize over her deed, completely unaware of what provoked her. A Beast Trait/Path check may be in order. This power works on both supernatural creatures and mortals, and requires you to kiss the victim (a Physical Challenge may be in order — remember, no touching) and defeat her in a Mental Test. Willpower may not be used to negate the effects of this power. This power lasts one night per Mental Trait invested into the initial challenge or until the death of the target's victim.

Dominate

Master

Obedience

You may now use all other *Dominate* Disciplines without eye contact. To activate this power, all you need to do is be able to see and talk to the target. (And yes, you must actually speak to the target, and have the target understand. "Within earshot" doesn't cut it.)

Rationale

Those whom you *Dominate* are convinced their actions are entirely of their own design, and were right and proper under the circumstances. This power requires a successful Mental Challenge against the target to work. If you are successful, the target believes that whatever he did under the influence of your successful *Dominate* Challenge was done of his own volition. The effects last for one evening.

Fortitude

Master

Imperviousness

Your ability to shrug off most forms of damage has reached unbelievable heights. You may perform a Simple Test to negate nonaggravated wounds; you conduct one test per wound incurred. If you win, you take no damage.

Invulnerability

You have become a walking juggernaut. Only the most tenacious and cunning of opponents stand a chance of bringing you down. You may perform a Simple Test to negate aggravated wounds; you conduct one test per wound level incurred. If you win, you take no damage; on a tie the wound becomes nonaggravated.

You cannot continue testing down with *Imperviousness* after a successful test on *Invulnerablility*.

Melpominee

Basic

The Missing Voice

You may "throw" your voice, causing to it emanate from any place within view. This operates independently of you, and you may continue to talk normally while the "thrown" voice chimes in. This power works automatically, but if you wish to undertake any other actions at the same time, you must perform a Mental Challenge; success indicates you can divide your concentration. The best way to handle this is to give a Narrator a note with what you wish to say.

Master
Art's Traumatic Essence

You may now drive others mad with the sound of your voice. To affect the target, you must win a Social Challenge against her. Once affected, the target gains a random Derangement (as determined by the Storyteller) for the remainder of the evening. Both characters are aware of what the Derangement is and may act accordingly. This Discipline can only affect one target at a time, unless the Daughter of Cacophany spends a Willpower Trait. Each Trait spent thus allows for an additional victim.

Mytherceria

Basic (level 2)
Darkling Trickery

This power allows the Kiasyd to play minor magical pranks. By defeating a target in a Mental Challenge, you can create spontaneous effects. While none of them should be overtly harmful, they most certainly should be annoying to the victim. Examples of possible effects: target lets out a deafening scream, target slips and falls, target's gun jams, target's pants fall down, target sneezes steadily for one minute straight. The effect of this power should be regulated closely by a Narrator.

Master
Riddle Phantastique

By defeating the target in a Mental Challenge, this Discipline allows you to recite a riddle of your choosing. The target can then do nothing but try to solve it, although she may defend herself as normal if attacked. The Riddle is so impenetrable that it can actually damage the minds that think about it. The target must try to guess the answer to the riddle once every 10 minutes, whether she knows the answer or not. For every incorrect guess made by the target, she takes one nonaggravated wound. Every third incorrect guess results in the target receiving an aggravated wound. Malkavians or Kindred with two or more Derangements are immune to this side effect. The duration of this power is one night, or until completion of the riddle.

Earth Sword

This power allows you to cause huge spikes to shoot out of walls, ceilings and floors. The spikes will be made of the same material as the surface from which they form, and can be especially dangerous to vampires in a wooden house or room. An attack of this nature is considered a ranged attack, and requires a challenge of your Mental Traits versus the target's Physical Traits. If the attack is successful, the target suffers two levels of nonaggravated damage. Wooden spikes that damage Kindred are accompanied by a Simple Test to see if the target has been staked. Due to the huge size of the spikes, only one Simple Test need be made. (Note: This is *not* a physical test of brute strength on the target's part, so *Potence* cannot be used in the challenge.)

Necromancy

Basic

Insight

This Discipline allows you to look into the eyes of a corpse and view the last five minutes those eyes saw in life, often images of the target's killer and the manner of death. *Insight* also works on the walking dead, and may allow you to perceive the identity of a vampire's sire. A Mental Challenge must be won if the target resists.

Master

Torment

By expending a Willpower Trait and winning a Simple Test, you may initiate Physical Challenges to strike and physically harm wraiths for 10 minutes as if you were beyond the Shroud. The wraith cannot escape by becoming incorporeal, nor can the ghost strike you, because you are not in the Shadowlands. A wraith reduced to zero Corpus goes through a Harrowing as described in **Oblivion**.

Spirit Possession

You now possess the power to place wraiths within the bodies of the dead. After summoning a wraith, you may expend a Willpower Trait to place it, if willing, into a dead body. The wraith may then inhabit the body for up to one week. (Note: A wraith placed in a body this way does not become a Risen — see **Oblivion**.) You may attempt to place a wraith in a Kindred body; however, you must spend two Willpower Traits and win a Mental Challenge against the owner of the body. The spirit of the ousted vampire may initiate one Mental Challenge per day against the wraith to regain control of his body. A vampire exiled from his body becomes a semi-wraith and his former body is now his one and only Fetter as described in **Oblivion**. A wraith possessing a Kindred body has full access to any *Celerity*, *Fortitude* or *Potence* Disciplines the vampire may have had.

Obeah

Basic (Level 2)

Anesthetic Touch

By using this power, you may lay your hands on someone and stop her body from feeling any pain, or bring a vampire out of frenzy. This power also paralyzes the target for one turn per Mental Trait expended. You must defeat an unwilling target in a Physical Challenge. Improper use of this Discipline (e.g., using this power simply to paralyze a target) may demand a Beast Trait check.

Master

Pain for Pleasure

By spending a Willpower Trait, you can dull the senses of your target such that he feels intense pleasure instead of pain and suffers no Trait penalties for wounds. Unfortunately, this also results in the target not realizing he is injured. The experience is very sensual, and some targets have been known to injure themselves deliberately to achieve the sensation again.

Vitae Block

This power allows you to render a portion of another vampire's blood inert and unusable. By succeeding in a Mental Challenge, you spend a Mental Trait for every Blood Trait you wish to block. The target may only use those "blocked" Blood Traits after he spends an equal number of Willpower Traits. Although spending Willpower may be done one Trait at a time until the task is completed, none of the blocked vitae will be usable until it is all freed.

Obfuscate

Master

Cloak the Aura

With this power, you can completely cloak your aura from the prying eyes of others. By expending a Willpower Trait, you can completely conceal your aura or change it at will. Others attempting to use *Aura Perception*, *Telepathy* or *Soul Scan* on you must defeat you in an opposed Mental Challenge to break the Cloak. If the Cloak is broken, your opponent must defeat you in an additional Mental Challenge for any of the previous powers to have an effect.

Cloak the Aura's effects override those of any lesser *Obfuscate* power.

Conceal

Similar to the Intermediate power *Cloak the Gathering*, you may now enshroud nonliving objects, up to but no larger than the size of a house. You must decide the number of Mental Traits you wish to invest in the concealment. The invested Traits determine the rating of the Static Challenge for any opponents who wish to pierce the concealment. Once active, the effects of this power are permanent until broken.

Obtenebration

Master

Eyes of the Night

With the expenditure of a Mental Trait, you are able to see anything that goes on within the dark force created by any other use of this Discipline. Thus you could evoke *Eyes of the Night* in another room and clairvoyantly scan the area within. Moreover, you may use this power to view your surroundings from any angle or vantage point within 50 feet of your body where a shadow exists. You only perceive visual information through use of this power. Using this power requires the expenditure of a Mental Trait per five minutes of use.

Shadow Step

With the expenditure of two Mental Traits you can walk into one shadow and exit from another up to 50 feet away. This power acts as a limited form of teleportation. You may use it to bypass solid walls, ascend a floor in a building, and get around other obstacles. You may also attempt to pull others through a shadow by reaching into the shadow, grabbing the victim and pulling her through to your own location (this requires a Physical Challenge). You may carry objects through the shadows (including living creatures). Use of this power requires you to state which shadow you wish to step through, then to walk over the stated shadow from which you wish to exit and then resume play. Use of this power is a Fair Escape.

Potence

Master

Force

Your supernatural strength has reached proportions that are the stuff of legend. You amaze fellow Kindred as you heft cars from the street, and are able to grind coal into diamonds with your bare hands. So devastating is your immense strength that in physical confrontations opponents must now defeat you in two tests instead of one. If either test is lost, your opponent takes damage. If your opponent is using *Force*, and if each of you wins one of the tests, you both take full damage.

Demolition

You now possess power so colossal that only the suicidal or the insane would cross you in a test of strength. You are so dangerous in hand-to-hand combat you inflict two additional wounds if you win the challenge. If your opponent uses *Demolition*, and if each of you wins one of the tests, you both take full damage.

Presence

Master

Love

This power duplicates the effect of a Blood Bond for as long as the target is in your presence. You must win a Social Challenge for this Discipline to take effect.

Mind Numb

This power allows you to cause those around you (up to, but not exceeding five targets) to lose all feeling, emotion and any motivation for action. After choosing the group affected, you must expend a Willpower Trait, then conduct a Social Challenge against each member in the group. If you are successful, all affected targets will tend to do nothing. Some may continue to perform rote tasks, such as vacuuming or stirring, if they were doing so just before *Mind Numb* took affect. The targets react to nothing but simple and immediate input, such as hot objects put in their hands. They will not be frightened if put in danger, or become angry if they are yelled at. This effect lasts as long as you are in their presence. Any direct action intended to cause physical harm to the target breaks the hold.

Protean

Flesh of Marble

Your skin has become as hard as stone, but loses none of its flexibility. It is now almost impossible to cut you, stake you, or do lasting physical damage to you. Opponents must defeat you in three successive tests to stake you (in addition to winning the necessary Physical Challenge). A character with *Flesh of Marble* doubles his Health Levels with regard to wounds of a physical nature. *Flesh of Marble* would not block such Disciplines as *Death of the Drum*, *Cauldron of Blood*, etc.

Form of the Ghost

While similar to *Mist Form* in that you become insubstantial, *Form of the Ghost* allows you to retain your own form and to move at a normal pace. Gravity and the elements (except fire and sunlight) do not affect you normally, henceforth giving you a version of flight. In addition, solid objects have no effect on you, and you may pass through them at will. You may not physically manipulate objects in the solid world. You must expend a Blood Trait to enter this form, which may be left at will. The transformation into *Form of the Ghost* is instantaneous and in some situations may give a Fair Escape. When you are employing this power, you cannot touch or be touched by another character employing this power. While in this form you are still affected by wards, and can utilize any Discipline that does not require touch.

Quietus

Basic

Weakness

With this power, you can utilize your blood as a contact poison. Flesh-to-flesh contact, the expenditure of a Blood Trait and a successful Physical Challenge are all required to use *Weakness*. If the attempt is successful, the victim is down two Physical Traits for an hour.

Master

Taste of Death

You may now spit a Trait's worth of blood at your foes, doing aggravated damage to those you hit. An attack of this form is considered a ranged attack; therefore, you may use Mental Traits to defend against your target's Physical Traits. You may spit blood 10 feet for every two Physical Traits you possess.

Foul Blood

By expending a Willpower Trait, you permanently make the blood of a vessel undrinkable and vile to anyone but yourself. Anyone who drinks the blood of a tainted vessel must spend the next minute vomiting profusely, and takes one nonaggravated wound per Blood Trait consumed.

Serpentis

Master

Temptation

You can attempt to tempt the target into evil actions (e.g., murder, slander, thievery, etc.) by simply speaking with her and telling her about her weakness. If the target is visibly upset at another character, you may initiate a Social Challenge to implant a suggestion in the target's mind regarding that character that the target will attempt to carry out at all costs. You may not spend Willpower Traits in the normal fashion to negate the effects of *Temptation*. Willpower Traits may be spent over time to stave off its effects. It takes a total of eight Willpower Traits to negate the effects of *Temptation*. The target may be induced to perform actions that cause her to receive Beast or Path Traits.

Obsession

This power inspires the target with an overpowering lust for a certain substance or condition as dictated by you. You need only speak with the target, telling her about this "lust" and defeat her in a Social Challenge. Whether the desire in question be money, sex or power, the target will crave it uncontrollably. The target must possess or experience the object of her desire at least once during the night, or she will frenzy when the game session nears its end (dictated by the Narrator). The target may try to stave off the *Obsession* once per night by winning a Static Challenge against her own total Mental Traits. To permanently rid herself of the *Obsession* she must expend a total of nine Willpower Traits. With this Discipline, the target may be induced to perform actions that cause her to receive Beast or Path Traits.

Spiritus

Basic

Summon Spirit Beasts

You can call on the spirits of dead animals to aid you. These spirits will be predisposed to helping you, and can follow simple telepathic com-

mands. The spirits can take any action of which they were capable in normal life (e.g., a bird spirit can fly, a dog spirit has keen hearing, etc.). Generally it takes one Mental Trait to summon a spirit, but a Narrator may issue a higher cost for a larger, more powerful spirit. The spirit arrives in 10-30 minutes. No one can see the spirit companion except those who have powers that enable them to see into the spirit world. The spirit will aid you for one night, and then return to the land of the dead.

Master
Engling Fury
You may now feed off an animal spirit to replenish all your lost Willpower Traits. Use of this power destroys the spirit, however, and may only be invoked once per session. After using this Discipline, you may not access any other *Spiritus* powers for the remainder of the night.

Spirit Form
With this power you can transform yourself into the spiritual form of any natural animal not larger than a bear and no smaller than a hummingbird. In many respects this power works similarly to the *Protean* Discipline *Shadow of the Beast*. In this form you appear as a ghostly version of the animal in question; however, you are actually a solid creature which can attack and be wounded normally. The change only alters your body and normal clothes; other equipment, including weapons, are unchanged. To activate this power you must expend a Blood Trait. This power takes one action to activate. You gain extra Physical Traits while in this spirit form, depending on its size. As a small creature (e.g., a bird or a bat), you gain the Physical Traits *Quick* and *Lithe*. As a medium creature (e.g., a wolf or a dog), you gain the Physical Traits *Ferocious* x 2 and *Vigorous*. If you assume the form of a large creature (e.g., a bear or a tiger), you gain the Physical Traits *Ferocious*, *Rugged*, *Stalwart* and *Tough*.

Thanatosis

Basic (Level 2)
Hag's Wrinkles
With the expenditure of a Blood Trait, you may expand or contract your skin, allowing you to change both your general appearance and apparent age. This ability can also be used to conceal small items in your body by creating pockets of flesh that are then tightly sealed.

Master

Compress

By expending three Blood Traits and defeating the target in a Physical Challenge, you can cause the your opponent's skin to shrink until it ruptures, causing two aggravated wounds. If the attack succeeds, you can then "absorb" your victim's skin into your own body, gaining three Physical Traits (*Resilient, Tough, Vigorous*) for the remainder of the night.

Dust to Dust

This power is similar in appearance to the Intermediate Discipline *Ashes to Ashes*, but is much more potent. Once you opt to transform into a pile of heavy ashes, you retain complete control over all mental Disciplines except *Dominate* and *Thaumaturgy*. The dust cannot be forced apart or moved by the wind unless you so desire. You can also use winds to aid movement while in this form. Like characters employing the *Form of Mist*, you retain cohesion without difficulty. To enter this form requires the expenditure of two Physical Traits.

Thaumaturgy

Path of Conjuring

Nothing larger or heavier than the conjurer may be summoned (no LAW rockets and no tanks). Conjured items differ from their "live" counterparts in that they seem too perfect and have no distinguishing characteristics.

Basic

Summoning the Spirit

You can summon a simple inanimate object with the expenditure of one Willpower Trait. The object cannot be more complex than a hand-held object with no moving parts (dagger, pencil) and weighing no more than 10 pounds. The object remains solid for 10 minutes for every Willpower Trait expended (e.g., three Willpower equals 30 minutes), then returns to the place from which it was summoned.

Permanency

You can conjure an object without the expense of Willpower. The object cannot be more complex than a hand-held object with no moving parts (dagger, pencil). An object conjured in this fashion is permanent and must be physically returned to its place of origin. The cost for this power is the expenditure of two Blood Traits.

Intermediate

Magic of the Smith

You can summon forth complex objects with moveable parts (handguns, CD players, anything within the limits of size) with the expenditure of two Willpower Traits. You must have a working knowledge (Storyteller's discretion) of the object. The object remains for 10 minutes per every Willpower Trait you expend (e.g., three Willpower points equals 30 minutes). *Permanency* will not affect objects conjured with this power.

Advanced

Power Over Life

You may create simple simulacra of living beings. These creations lack free will, emotions and creativity, but will follow your orders. To conjure the simulacra requires the expenditure of five Blood Traits. The beings last for one evening and may not be made permanent. (Note: Simulacra [or golems] created in this way have seven Physical Traits, no Mental or Social Traits, no Abilities, and are immune to all Mental and Social Challenges.)

Spirit Thaumaturgy

Failures in *Spirit Thaumaturgy* are not recommended; the spirit of a botched summoning may turn out to be a Spectre or may decide to follow the vampire around for a while to harass her. This is the rarest Path of *Thaumaturgy*; most of its practitioners learned the rudiments as mortals. This Path is known among Sabbat and Camarilla Tremere.

Basic

Evil Eye

You can summon a wraith to harass a victim for a duration of time determined by the number of Mental Traits expended into the challenge. You must defeat the victim in a Mental Challenge. If you are successful, the victim must bid two extra Traits in any challenges for 10 minutes. You may extend the duration of harassment at the cost of one Mental Trait per five minutes.

Spirit Eyes

You may attempt to see and communicate with wraiths in the area. A successful Mental Challenge versus the wraith is required before you are able to see or communicate with it. You may communicate with the ghost for five minutes for every Mental Trait you expend.

Intermediate

Spirit Slave

This power allows you to master a summoned wraith. To use this power, you must win a Mental Challenge against the wraith. If you win the test, the wraith is bound to remain and answer any questions you like, or perform any one task you require. If unwilling, the wraith might opt to perform the task poorly. An additional use of this power can force a recently dead wraith into permanently haunting the present location. This effect requires a successful Mental Challenge against the target. However, this effect can (at the Storyteller's discretion) eventually wear off.

Journey

This power is similar to the *Auspex* power of *Psychic Projection*, but your spirit remains within the physical realm. Your body remains in one place while the spirit travels around. You can be trapped inside fetishes when in this state, and can potentially be controlled by any spirit power. Mental Disciplines that do not require touch are available for use while in this state, with the exception of *Necromancy* or any other *Spirit Thaumaturgy*. Any power requiring physical contact or that manipulates the physical body is unavailable. Your spirit is visible to those around you unless *Obfuscate* is being used. To activate this power requires the expenditure of one Willpower Trait. While in this form, your spirit is immune to physical harm but is affected by sunlight and wards as normal.

Advanced

Fetishes

You can cause spirits to inhabit objects, or fetishes, which you may then carry around with you. Once the spirit is imprisoned, the fetish will allow you access to one and only one power (not to exceed Advanced level) that the spirit possesses. The power that becomes available is determined by the Storyteller. A successful Mental Challenge against the victim is all that is required to bind the spirit to the fetish. The spirit is trapped in the fetish until the fetish is broken. Before you may access any power of the fetish, you must permanently expend a Mental Trait to attune the item to yourself.

Elemental Mastery

Basic

Elemental Strength

This power allows you to increase your Physical Traits without the need to expend Blood Traits. You can expend one Willpower Trait to gain the Physical Traits *Brawny, Dexterous* and *Resilient*. To maintain this power, you must continue to expend one Willpower Trait per round after the first round. You may only spend one Willpower Trait per round toward this Discipline.

Wooden Tongues

This power allows you to gain information from inanimate objects. You may attempt to gain impressions of what the object has experienced by succeeding in a static Mental Challenge against the object (difficulty determined by Storyteller). The object's memories are limited and its feelings may be completely alien to you, but any information gained can be extremely valuable. This use of the Discipline usually requires the assistance of a Narrator. To enact this power, you must expend a Mental Trait.

Intermediate

Animate the Unmoving

This power allows you to animate objects that are within line of sight. With the expenditure of one Willpower Trait and a successful Static Challenge, you can call upon an object to perform a simple task. Chairs can run, statues can walk or attack, and a stake could squirm out of someone's hand. You may keep the object active past the first round at the cost of one Mental Trait per extra round. The Narrator should determine the Traits of the object.

Elemental Form

With the expenditure of one Blood Trait, you can assume the form of an inanimate object of equal size and weight to your own (e.g., a chair, desk, pillar, etc.). You may opt also to spend one Willpower Trait at the time of change, which allows you to have access to your senses and Disciplines. There is no cost to return to your original form.

Advanced

Summon Elemental

This power allows you to beckon one of the traditional elementals of myth (fire, water, air and earth). You must succeed in a Static

Disciplines and Rituals

Mental Challenge against 10 Traits to summon the elemental. Then you must win a Simple Test to control the creature. If you fail the Simple Test, the elemental attacks you. If it is controlled, you may banish the elemental at will. See **Laws of the Wild** for the statistics of the elementals. The duration of this power is one hour.

Corruption

All of these powers require that the target be within arm's reach of the caster. Setites cannot learn this Path without first learning the Path of Blood.

Basic

Contradict

You can make the target say or do the opposite of her intended action. A left turn becomes a right turn, or a yes becomes no. You must defeat the target in a Mental Challenge to have this effect.

Disfigurement

This Discipline allows you to make minor changes to a target's facial features for the night. You could remove eyebrows, lengthen the target's nose, or enlarge her ears. This ability is not powerful enough to disguise an individual completely or even to make the target unrecognizable. You must succeed in a Mental Challenge against the target. If you are successful, the target receives the Negative Trait *Repulsive* x 2 for the remainder of the evening.

Intermediate

Change Mind

You can change the Demeanor of your target for the evening. The victim is affected by drastic mood swings immediately, as her Demeanor changes to your choice. This power requires a successful Mental Challenge.

Cripple

This power allows you to turn your victim into an invalid for a round. The target may not initiate Physical Challenges and must bid three extra Traits in any Physical Challenge initiated against her. You must expend a Willpower Trait and win a Mental Challenge against the victim. For each level of *Fortitude* the target possesses, you must expend an additional Mental Trait. You may opt to extend the time of affliction at a cost of one Mental Trait per minute.

Advanced

Corrupt Soul

After the expenditure of a Willpower Trait in addition to a successful Mental Challenge, you can change your target's Nature for the evening. This ability is a more intense version of *Change Mind* and can warp the victim's very essence.

Vicissitude

Master

Body Arsenal

You can use your own body to create weapons. You can manifest claws similar to the *Protean* power *Wolf's Claws*, but this power goes far beyond that. By expending a Blood Trait and investing one Mental Trait per Physical Trait of the weapon (up to but not exceeding three Traits) you may can create any melee weapon you can imagine (i.e., sword, club, dagger, whip, etc.) from your flesh. No projectile weapons can be created by the use of this power. Weapons thus created inflict aggravated wounds. Note: This power never allows more than a three-Trait bonus at any one time, nor does it add to the Traits one acquires by switching to Horrid Form.

Plasmic Form

You can turn parts of your body to blood and then reform them later. You choose what parts of your body to turn to blood. If you so desire, you may manipulate the blood once it has been created. You can move any or all of the blood, and travel through cracks, under doors, etc. You are immune to all physical attacks other than fire and sunlight while in this form. You can travel as a pool of red liquid or appear completely normal except for the red coloration (although you will still be a mass of blood held in a bipedal form by surface tension). In this state you can speak and walk normally.

When in this form, your body parts are not solid to bullets and fists splash harmlessly through you. You will not be able to "hit" anyone, drink blood or engage in other physical activity except as noted above. You may only use Mental and Social Disciplines while in this form. To activate this power you must expend two Blood Traits.

Disciplines and Rituals

Visceratika

Kindred of the Gargoyle bloodline are the only vampires who can possess this Discipline.

Basic

Skin of the Chameleon

By expending a Blood Trait, you can make your skin take on the texture of your surroundings. By standing still or moving very slowly (one step per three seconds) you blend in so well you cannot be seen by normal eyes. Characters with *Heightened Senses* may opt to do a Mental Challenge against your Physical Traits to find you. (Note: Unlike *Unseen Presence*, this power is not a trick of the mind and does not cause characters to actively avoid your location.) You may move and speak while utilizing this power, but its usefulness is nullified at that point.

Whispers of the Chamber

With the expenditure of a Willpower Trait, you are able to attune yourself to detect intruders within an enclosed area. The area can be as large as a small apartment (about 30' by 30') with which you are intimately familiar. This power works even if the intruders are out of sight, in darkness or protected by *Obfuscate*. If the target is actively seeking to avoid being detected, a Mental Challenge versus the target is in order.

Intermediate

Voices of the Castle

As *Whispers of the Chamber*, but affecting an entire building or physical structure.

Advanced

Bond with Terra

Similar to the *Protean* power *Earth Meld*, this power allows you to melt into stone, brick or asphalt. However, this power does not allow you to sink deep into the protective surroundings. Instead, you seep just below the surface and a faint outline of your form can be seen above where you rest. This power protects from both fire and the sun. If an adversary attempts to harm you, the surrounding rock effectively gives you five extra Healthy Traits. This power requires the expenditure of a Blood Trait.

Master

Stonestrength

Your flesh hardens and takes on a very distinct rocklike quality. Every manifestation of this power is different in appearance. For some it results in a look of polished marble, while others resemble rough granite. Your skin becomes rock hard and pain is deadened, giving you the extra Physical Trait *Tough* (above and beyond the maximum allowed by generation). You are immune to wound penalties and take only half damage from fire.

Rockheart

Your innards become rocklike. You are considered to have double Health Levels against physical attacks that do piercing or smashing damage. To stake you, your attacker must at least have *Puissance*. (Note: If this power is used in conjunction with *Flesh of Marble* no extra Health Levels are gained, but it now takes three tests to stake you.)

Rituals

Basic

Blood Walk

This ritual allows you to trace the lineage of a subject. By winning a Simple Test, you may learn the identity of the target's sire. You can continue testing in order to learn successive ancestors, though a single failure ends the ritual. Each successive test requires the same time investment as the initial ritual.

Calling the Restless Spirit

By enacting this ritual, you can summon up a ghost for five minutes of conversation after succeeding on a Simple Test. Any interruption ends the conversation. You must be within 10 feet of the corpse, or in the area of a haunting in the case of wraiths. This power gives you no control over the spirit in question, who is not required to do the summoner's bidding. This will work on a vampire who has died the Final Death, but not through diablerie.

Donning the Mask of Shadows

By casting this ritual, you are able to conceal yourself in shadows, much as the *Obfuscate* power *Unseen Presence*. For each Mental Trait invested, you have the ability to become invisible for one hour. All benefits and liabilities for *Unseen Presence* apply.

Disciplines and Rituals

Mourning Life Curse

This one-hour ritual may be prepared ahead of time, requiring crocodile blood, and completed before the end of the evening. By whispering the final word in the ear of a mortal, you cause said mortal to cry tears of blood. There is no known defense, and the victim will continue to bleed until the caster breaks the line of sight. The effect is not painful, but could greatly disturb a victim. The bleeding is slow, causing loss of one Blood Trait per every five minutes. As well as normal after-effects of blood loss, the subject's eyes will be bloodshot.

Principal Focus of Vitae Infusion

You are able to alter an object so as to hold a Blood Trait. The object must be able to fit into your hands, but no smaller than a pea. After receiving the Blood Trait, the object becomes reddish and slick. You can reclaim this blood by touching the object and willingly releasing it from its enchantment, causing the object to disintegrate and turn into the Blood Trait. Another Kindred may be incorporated into the ritual, allowing him to claim the Blood Trait, but he must be present during the initial casting. The Blood Trait used is still yours. This ritual takes four hours to cast. Blood contained in this manner will not spoil as other blood does.

Rite of Introduction

This ritual allows you to announce yourself to all Tremere within a city. After performing the ritual, which requires speaking into a cloud of water vapor, you may speak with a recipient for five minutes for every Mental Trait expended. This starts with the Regent of the chantry within the city and progresses to the others according to their knowledge of *Thaumaturgy*, from greatest to least. The casting allows you to write down a short introduction which is then given to all Tremere. If a conversation is then desired by one of the city residents, you must expend a Mental Trait before you may speak. Only one person may be spoken to at a time; traditionally, only the Regent replies to the announcement.

Unless the player can produce an overwhelming reason not to select this Rite as her basic ritual, characters should default to Rite of Introduction.

Rebirth of Mortal Vanity

This simple ritual allows you to grow hair after the Embrace. It is also usable on others. A hair from a different mortal child is required for each inch of hair growth desired. It can be useful in facilitating disguises.

Scent of the Garou's Passing

Smelling a mixture of wolfsbane, milkweed and some more arcane foul-smelling ingredients will allow you to detect the presence of a Garou. A Mental Challenge must be won against the target, and you can only identify Garou that you have previously smelled before. You are able to determine the following things: gender, time of passage and breed.

The Open Passage

This ritual takes 10 minutes and a Blood Trait to cast. The caster traces an intricate design upon a barrier, such as a stone wall, which will then become insubstantial for the purpose of allowing someone to pass through. The ritual only lasts for one minute.

Wake with Morning's (Evening's) Freshness

This ritual must be performed immediately prior to going to sleep for the day. Complete meditation is required. Any interruption, or the performance of other activities after the ritual but before going to sleep, renders the ritual null and void. At any sign of danger during the day, you will immediately awaken. You will be able to act normally, as if it were night, except for being able to go into the sun. Feathers must be burned and spread over the sleeping area to cast this ritual. Also, you must spend a Mental Trait to get the proper meditation.

Intermediate

Binding the Beast

This 10-minute ritual will remove a Kindred from frenzy, separating him from his Beast for a short while. You need not see the subject; merely drink one Blood Trait from the frenzying character (which could have been obtained earlier), and push an iron spike through the palm of your hand, causing a normal wound. Upon completion, the target immediately emerges from frenzy and becomes extremely passive, gaining the Negative Traits *Submissive* x 2 for the remainder of the night.

Bladed Hands

This ritual requires you to expend a Blood Trait and takes 10 minutes to cast. Upon doing so you gain the bonus Physical Trait *Sharp* until next sunrise. Be careful when handling fragile objects or touching people; a handshake could be dangerous.

Disciplines and Rituals

Eyes of the Past

By expending two Mental Traits and casting this ritual, you are able to view events at the location of the casting, up to five years prior. A specific time and date must be chosen. Up to a five-minute time span can be watched, and during this full sensory enchantment, you will be unaware of your physical surroundings. This ritual may only affect one room.

Flesh of Fiery Touch

This protective ritual causes your skin to become a lethal trap. Anyone who lays bare hands upon your skin will be burned. This ritual lasts until the next nightfall. For each touch, or once per turn for continued touches, the target takes one aggravated wound. Casually brushing against someone will not cause damage, nor will your clothes be set aflame. This ritual is not without its drawbacks. During this two-hour ritual, you must spend a Willpower Trait, and swallow a burning coal, which inflicts an aggravated wound. This can be reduced with *Fortitude* or healed as normal. While you are enchanted, your skin has a noticeable bronze tint and feels hot to anyone touching it. The effect works only for skin on skin — even a thin layer of clothing destroys the effect.

Gentle Mind

With this ritual, you are able to bestow an extra two Willpower Traits upon the subject for the purpose of resisting frenzy. You and the target must exchange one Blood Trait each, consuming one from the subject in order to cast this ritual; the caster may never cast this on himself. The extra Willpower Trait can only be used to resist frenzy and nothing else. The duration of this ritual is one night.

Haunted House

This ritual may be cast on any Kindred's haven. After casting, rumors begin to circulate of the location being haunted, leading many to shun it. Even those who profess disbelief will avoid the place. You must spend three Blood Traits to cast this ritual, with more Blood Traits increasing the effect. The ritual will last for 10 years, at which time, mortals will begin to rationalize the place as merely run-down or just weird. Most vampires treat this ritual as a breach of the Masquerade.

Heart of Stone

By casting this ritual, your heart turns to solid stone, leaving you immune to staking. The ritual requires an earthen circle three inches high and six feet in diameter to be formed on a natural stone surface (poured stone, such as concrete, is not acceptable). You must lie prone in the center and place a lighted candle directly over your heart, allowing it to burn down. This causes one aggravated wound. The ritual will last as long as the caster desires, dispelled with a thought. While under this enchantment, you cannot spend Willpower. If you are forced to spend Willpower, the ritual ends immediately. While under the effects of this ritual, you lose all *Friendly* or *Compassionate* Social Traits, and gain a number of *Callous* Negative Social Traits equal to half your remaining allotment of Social Traits.

Illusion of Peaceful Death

This ritual heals visible wounds on a corpse, making it appear as if the person has died of natural causes. It does not add blood to a corpse, but will remove reasons for a person to check for blood loss. At least half of a full Blood Pool must be in the body for this ritual to work. You must "dust" the corpse with a white feather and expend two Mental Traits.

Innocence of the Child's Heart

This ritual hides your aura from *Aura Perception*. Anyone using that Discipline successfully upon you sees a white aura, devoid of any signs of vampirism. A mortal child's toy must be carried throughout the duration of the ritual, which lasts for one hour per Mental Trait invested at the time of the casting.

Protean Curse

The target of this ritual is turned into a bat, as with the Protean Discipline *Form of the Beast*. The target must drink a Blood Trait taken from a rabid vampire bat. If the target is unwilling, the caster must defeat him in a Physical Challenge. This ritual affects only Kindred and humans, and lasts only one night.

Rending Sweet Earth

With this ritual you can open a 10-foot by 10-foot opening into the earth, leading to an *Earth Melded* vampire. If the *Earth Melded* Kindred is asleep, he is automatically awakened, but will not do so if in torpor. The ritual must be cast exactly where the vampire entered the ground. The caster strikes the ground repeatedly with a leather whip and must defeat the subject in a Mental Challenge. If the target is in torpor, the ritual automatically works. The effect lasts only for a single night.

The Unseen Change

This ritual requires marking an area with wolf's blood poured from a silver jug and investing a number of Mental Traits. Any Garou entering the area must win a Static Mental Challenge, difficulty determined by the number of invested Traits, or be forced to automatically change to Lupus form and stay that way while within the circle. Once activated, the ritual remains in effect for one evening.

The Watcher

This ritual summons a rat, who then goes wherever the caster directs and looks for whatever the caster indicates. When the rat returns, the caster may touch its head and see what it has seen. The caster may even have the rat steal small objects, but she must be exacting in detail about the object's appearance and location to avoid mistakes. You must win a Static Social Challenge, the difficulty determined by the number of rats nearby, in order to cast this ritual. It lasts until next sunrise. The summoned rat is still subject to *Animalism* Disciplines.

Advanced

Blood Contract

Using a Blood Trait, you create a binding agreement between two parties. If either party willingly breaches the agreement, the result is Final Death of he who broke the pact. Both parties must use a Blood Trait to sign the agreement. The only way to dissolve the commitment is to complete one's part of the contract, or to physically burn the agreement.

Curse of Clytaemnestra

Through use of this ritual, you are able to destroy one male mortal (including ghouls) by aging him rapidly, decaying him into nothing. You must have a personal possession of the subject, as well as at least one Blood Trait. The ritual takes one full day to cast. The target can resist by winning a Static Physical Challenge, the difficulty determined by the number of Blood Traits invested by the caster during the ritual. If the subject ties, then he is merely crippled and takes three normal wounds.

Stone Slumber

By casting this ritual, which must start two hours before dawn, you are turned into stone at sunrise. Similar to any other stone statue, you can be moved from place to place, even through sunlight, remaining

a statue until sunset. To rise from this form, three Blood Traits must be expended, as opposed to the normal one. You are immune to staking and most forms of fire. Pieces can be broken off, though, doing however much damage the Narrator decides. Most forms of communication are impossible, as the caster's mind is dormant. While in statue form, all of your Physical Traits are changed to *Enduring,* and you have double the Health Levels with regards to any physical damage attempted upon you. Activating this ritual requires the expenditure of two Mental Traits and a piece of rock broken off from another statue.

Clan Assamite Rituals

The Tremere are not the sole masters of *Thaumaturgy*. The Assamites have developed a number of rituals since their curse at the hands of the Tremere. You are required to have mastery of the appropriate level of the *Quietus* discipline to be able to learn one of these rituals of the same level.

Basic

Blood of Peace

A Blood Trait can be converted into a sleeping elixir with this ritual. It takes 10 minutes and two Blood Traits to cast this ritual. After the Blood Trait has been enchanted, it may be applied to a subject through ingestion or contact with the skin. You must then defeat the victim in a Mental Challenge; success indicates the target falls into a deep sleep which lasts for at least 10 minutes. Only extremely violent actions have a chance to wake a sleeper. This ritual works only on mortals.

Blood Call

Through use of this ritual you create a limited form of mental contact between yourself and another. Both parties involved must give two Blood Traits during the casting of the ritual, and then expend a permanent Mental Trait each. Afterward, if either party is destroyed, the other receives a vision containing the details of the demise.

Intermediate

Light of Vengeance

A focused artificial light source (such as a lamp or flashlight) can be changed into a weapon with almost the power of the sun. You must expend a Blood Trait and smear it on the light source. When you wish to attack someone with the light, you must win a Mental Challenge versus the target's Physical Traits. Success means that the target takes an aggravated wound. The ritual lasts until all of the Blood Traits smeared upon the light source are used up or until the end of the evening, when the blood is considered to have evaporated. Each successful attack burns a Blood Trait from the light source, and the attacks can only be directed at a single target.

Advanced

Healing Blood

The healing of aggravated wounds becomes much easier with the use of this ritual. Upon meditating for 10 minutes and expending two Mental Traits, you can heal an aggravated wound with only one Blood Trait, and no expenditure of Willpower. There is no limit to the number of aggravated wounds that may be healed in one night with the casting of this ritual, but all wounds to be healed at the less expensive cost must be healed immediately following this ritual. Any action other than healing aggravated wounds ends the ritual immediately.

Antitribu Rituals

Basic

Craft Bloodstone

Through this ritual, you may create a small mystical object called a Bloodstone. A Bloodstone acts as a magical beacon for the person to whom it is attuned. Once you have attuned a Bloodstone, you may sense its exact location in a nonvisual manner. This enchantment usually lasts for a century or so, although some have lasted for as long as 500 years. To create a Bloodstone, you must find a suitable stone and leave it within a container holding at least three Traits of your Blood for three nights. Each night you must chant over the container as the Bloodstone absorbs each Blood Trait. After the third night, the liquid within the container becomes clear like water. The ritual may be ended here, allowing you to sense the location of the Bloodstone wherever it is.

You can infuse more Blood Traits into the stone, at the rate of one each evening. These Blood Traits can be retrieved by anyone holding the Bloodstone at a rate of one per evening. You must win a Static Mental Challenge against a difficulty of five Traits each time the incantation is cast over the Bloodstone. This ritual can also be cast upon a pre-existing Bloodstone to attune it to you, as well as recharge it.

Eyes of the Nighthawk

This ritual allows you to receive the audio and visual information obtained by a bird. First you must touch the bird and feed it a specially prepared birdseed mixed with your blood. You must win a Static Mental Challenge against the bird (difficulty of five Traits). Upon success, you can then mentally control it, but where it will travel only. To receive information, you must close your eyes and concentrate; this action will leave you unaware of your current surroundings and unable to act until you break concentration. This ritual lasts for one month before it must be cast again.

Illuminate Trail of the Prey

Through the use of this ritual, you are able to view the trail of a target — footprints, tire tracks, airplane trajectories, etc. — as a glowing neon trail. However, the trail ends as soon as the target wades through or submerses himself in water. You must have viewed the target and have a starting point where the target has been in the past. The trail begins at the starting point, following the movements of the target, with the intensity of the glow being indirectly proportional to the amount of time which has passed since the target was present at the location. The caster must defeat the target in a Mental Challenge in order to track him.

Impassable Trail

By wrapping your feet in soft deerskin, you can pass through the thickest woods without leaving any visible trail. You must expend one dexterity-related Physical Trait to enact this ritual. The duration is an entire evening.

This Ritual works only in non-urban settings, though there are rumors that "advances" have been made allowing for the effects to function in even the heart of the urban jungle.

Machine Blitz

By casting this ritual, you can cause machines in the area to go haywire. You must expend a Mental Trait for each turn you desire this ritual to remain in effect. The enchantment allows machines a limited amount of movement, performing activity similar to their normal functions, even to the point of attacking whomever the caster desires. Any attacks use the caster's Mental Traits with a two-Trait penalty. The actual results should be determined between the involved parties, or by a Narrator.

Disciplines and Rituals

Power of the Invisible Flame

This simple ritual allows one who knows Path of the Flame to create invisible fires. The effects can be felt as normal, but aren't visible. The ritual lasts for one evening, and must be cast around a fire of at least torch size. Each time you wish to make invisible flames, you must expend a Mental Trait. You must have the Path of the Flame before you can learn this ritual.

Preserve Blood

By casting this ritual, you are able to prepare blood against spoiling, keeping it in a specially prepared earthenware container. The container must be prepared by burying it in earth for two nights. Thereafter, the container must be dug up. The blood is added, and the container is sealed with wax. Once opened, the blood spoils at a normal rate. You must win a Static Mental Challenge (difficulty of four Traits) in order to cast this ritual successfully.

Steps of the Terrified

This ritual allows you to slow down a specific target. You must win a Mental Challenge against the target. Afterward, each turn the victim tries to run she is slowed to half her speed. A normal run would only go half as far, while someone using *Celerity* would only get half as many actions as normal to run away, possibly slowing her down enough for lower levels of *Celerity* to catch her. As the victim tries to run each turn, she slows down by half again, eventually to a walk. The ritual requires a small cube of dried mud, perfectly square on all sides.

Summon Guardian Spirit

Through use of this ritual, you are able to summon a spirit for the next 24 hours to guard you. The spirit cannot do more than warn you of danger through interaction with the surrounding environment. It cannot speak and is only visible to you, and then only in times of danger. You cannot be surprised for the duration of the ritual. You must win a Static Social Challenge (difficulty of five Traits) to summon the spirit.

Will o' the Wisp

This simple ritual allows you to produce a supernatural light source. This ball of light can be mentally commanded to travel within your sight, and even perform simple tricks. The ball may become brighter, dimmer, separate into smaller balls, dart about, encompass someone in its glow, etc. It is most often used as a simple light source or diversion. A willow branch is required in the casting. This ritual will last as long as you concentrate on it. A Mental Trait must be expended each hour you wish the light to remain active.

Intermediate

Bottled Voice

By winning a Mental Challenge versus the target, speaking an incantation and gesturing toward an empty bottle, you are able to trap the target's voice within a bottle. The bottle must be sealed with wax in addition to any other closure, such as a cork. While the seal or bottle remains intact, the target cannot speak.

Eldritch Glimmer

By casting this ritual, you are able to surround yourself in a green glow. You can then throw fire bolts of this energy at a cost of one Blood Trait per bolt. These bolts inflict one aggravated wound, and may only be cast at the rate of one per turn. You must win a Mental Challenge versus the target's Physical Traits in order to hit. Each time a bolt is fired, you must win a Simple Test or expend a Mental Trait to keep the ritual from ending. The ritual's duration is only until the next dawn. This ritual requires a piece of sandstone soaked in vinegar.

Fire Walker

This ritual protects you from fire for up to an hour. Whenever you are attacked by fire and win a Simple Test, no damage is taken. A special salve must be rubbed on the soles of your feet, and two Mental Traits must be spent to cast this ritual.

Friend of the Trees

Anyone who tries to follow you through woods after you cast this ritual is immediately subject to interference from the surrounding foliage. These plants animate slightly, slowing down pursuers to half speed. You must plant an acorn and spend two Mental Traits to cast this ritual. It lasts as long as you remain in the woods or until the next sunrise.

The Haunting

By casting this ritual, you may summon a malevolent spirit to cause fear in a target. Like a poltergeist, this spirit will play tricks on a subject, but its intentions are to frighten, to death if it can. This spirit usually has little effect on Kindred, but it will make werewolves uneasy and frighten mortals. The spirit cannot directly harm the victim, but if it wins a Social Challenge against her, the spirit makes Simple Tests until it loses to determine how much harm it can do. One success freezes the target in place for a few minutes; two causes her to faint; three causes her to become Incapacitated. Four can kill the target unless she wins a Static Physical Challenge, the difficulty

Disciplines and Rituals

equal to the spirit's Social Traits. Survivors may awaken to find their hair turned white from the experience. Exactly what the spirit does and how long it haunt the victim is determined by the Narrator playing the spirit.

Keening of the Banshee

With a horrifying scream, you can cause the person nearest to you to age 13 years minus his total Physical Traits. His hair also turns white. You must win a Mental Challenge against the target in order to affect him. This ritual requires a necklace with a pendant carved from an old tombstone. This does nothing to Kindred but can harm mortals, ghouls and werewolves.

Mirror Walk

With this ritual, you are able to enter a mirror of a size big enough to crawl through. This allows you to use the mirror as a gate to the nearest mirror of large enough size to allow you access. You may safely take one person with you through the mirror. The mirror seems to liquefy, ripples cascading across the surface, returning to normal after you have gone through. You must be wearing a ring with an emerald when this ritual is in effect. If you are being chased, this ritual may be used as a Fair Escape. However, the pursuers, or anyone within five feet of the mirror when this is cast, may immediately state their intention to follow you through the mirror; otherwise the opportunity to follow is lost.

If the person does not come through the mirror willingly, she must win a Static Physical Challenge against a difficulty of 6 or be killed, one half of her lying in front of the entrance mirror and the other half lying in front of the exit mirror. You must expend three Mental Traits to enact this ritual.

Respect of the Animals

Through use of this ritual you are able to travel through wilderness areas without danger from animals. Animals neither like nor dislike you, but simply ignore you. Two Social Traits must be expended to enact this ritual, which lasts four hours.

Touch of Nightshade

This ritual gives you a touch that is literally fatal. After you have cast this ritual, the first mortal you touch must engage in a Physical Challenge with you. If he loses, he dies, instantly and painfully. If he ties, he is in severe pain from cramps for the rest of the evening, and is down two Traits in all tests during that time. Winning the Challenge allows the victim to avoid the effects, but he remains unaware of the attack. To

complete this ritual you must rub juice from some form of nightshade onto your hands. The attack is only good for a single target; the second mortal you touch after performing the ritual is safe from its effects.

Advanced

Dominion

This three-hour ritual, the effects of which last for a week, provides an effective defense against certain vampiric Disciplines. Proper casting of this ritual renders an area up to 500 square feet immune to all effects of *Animalism*, *Dominate* and *Presence*, except those you yourself create. Preparing the area properly mandates that iron seals be embedded over all doors within the area of effect, and they must remain so for the duration of the ritual's effect. If any of the seals are marred or removed, the effect ends instantly. You must expend three Mental Traits to cast this ritual.

Eyes of the Beast

Similar to *Eyes of the Nighthawk*, this ritual allows you to see through the eyes of any animal you have previously enchanted to serve as a conduit for the power. To prepare an animal properly, you must touch it on the forehead (not as easy as it sounds) and then win a Static Mental Challenge against seven Traits. Thereafter (at least for the duration of the ritual), you can close your eyes and, by concentrating, see through the enchanted beast's eyes. The ritual's effects last for six weeks, no matter how far the animal wanders from you. You may only cast this ritual on one animal at a time.

Lion Heart

By casting this ritual, you may increase your combat abilities. The ritual bestows upon you the Physical Traits *Brawny*, *Tough*, *Quick* and *Enduring*. When in a challenge that might cause you to flee, or be subject to a Fear frenzy, you gain an extra Willpower Trait. Finally, you also gain two Abilities in *Brawl* and two Abilities in *Leadership*. This ritual only lasts for 20 minutes. A Willpower Trait must be spent in order to enact this ritual. If you do not rest within two hours after the completion of this ritual, you will take one Health Level of damage for every 10 minutes you do not rest. The amount of time necessary to be considered rested is one hour.

Mindcrawler

An insidious force within a victim's mind is created by this ritual. You must place your hand upon a victim's head, which may require a Physical Challenge; the victim feels a slight burning sensation. For each day afterward, the victim loses one Mental Trait until all are lost. After all Mental Traits are lost, the ritual ceases. The victim may regain these lost Traits by putting forth effort in recovering them, at a rate of one Mental Trait per week. You must dye a small tick red, paint it with an arcane sigil, crush it, apply it to the victim's head, and then win a Mental Challenge against the target.

Paper Flesh

For one night, the victim of this ritual is bereft of most of the benefits of *Fortitude* and endurance-related Physical Traits. Victims of eighth generation or higher lose all but one endurance-related Physical Traits and *Fortitude* powers. With each succeeding generation, the victim hangs onto an additional Trait and *Fortitude* power.

In order to inflict *Paper Flesh* on a target, you must defeat her in a Mental Challenge and subsequently tear a picture of her in half.

Spirit of Torment

Similar to *The Haunting*, this ritual lets you summon a spirit to do your bidding. This time, the spirit is capable of taking on physical form and doing real damage to others.

In order to summon the spirit, you must win a Social Challenge. Once the challenge is won, the spirit obeys your commands to the letter, until to it takes damage to its physical form. At that point, the spirit flees.

The spirit has 13 Physical Traits, three Social Traits and seven Mental Traits. It has three Willpower Traits, the Abilities of *Brawl* x 4, *Intimidate* x 3 and *Occult*. It also has the following Disciplines: *Heightened Senses, Aura Perception, Might, Unseen Presence, Mask of 1000 Faces* and *Cloak the Gathering*. When trying to frighten someone, the spirit gains three bonus Social Traits (*Frightening* x 3). Furthermore, by winning a Mental Challenge, the spirit can see and identify anything in the local Near Umbra.

In its normal form, the spirit is incorporeal, but it can spend a Mental Trait in order to become corporeal for five minutes. The appearance, actions and other details of the spirit are left to the discretion of the Narrator.

Playing an Elder

Though you should be going to live three thousand years, and as many times ten thousand years, still remember that no one loses any other life than this which they now live, nor lives any other than this which they now lose.
— The Meditations of Marcus Aurelius, Book I

Symbols of Authority

Tonight it will finally happen: You will roleplay an elder Kindred in your game of **The Masquerade**. Your Storyteller agreed to let you take the plunge, and you spent the better portion of last night determining your character's Attribute Traits, Abilities, Influences and Disciplines. You relish the thought of entering tonight's session armed with enhanced powers, an increased number of Blood Traits and the ability to thumb your nose at any other Kindred who tries to use *Dominate* on you. You savor the thought of enforcing your character's every desire with the threat of serious retribution should anyone dare gainsay you, and you eagerly anticipate the first challenge to your authority. You are definitely ready for anything!

There is no denying that playing an elder Kindred can be a genuine adrenaline rush. Your character is, after all, one of the most powerful beings in the game, and there is little you could not accomplish through sheer force, threats or outright violence. But there is more — far more — to roleplaying an elder than increased character statistics and access to higher levels of your Disciplines. Portraying an elder can mean your greatest roleplaying challenge yet, a task which calls upon every ounce of skill you can muster. This is doubly true if you take the time to consider what being an elder vampire really *means* in the context of a game. In this chapter you will learn helpful hints about roleplaying an elder character convincingly, as well as advice on interacting with other characters. Most importantly, you will come to understand the very real responsibilities inherent in your role as an elder, and the necessity of recognizing the benefits of cooperative roleplaying to enhance **The Masquerade** experience for everyone involved.

Defining the Role — Who Are the Elders?

I am a brother to dragons, and a companion to owls. My skin is black upon me, and my bones are burned with heat.
— Job 30: 29-30

The fledgling Kindred nightly finds herself beset on all sides by dangers both numerous and lethal. Warring vampire sects vie for her loyalty, lawless anarchs seek her precious vitae, and master manipulators pull her strings from the shadows. Seductive compliments artfully camouflage a bewildering array of offers and counteroffers. Polite conversations mask honeyed promises of grand rewards and veiled threats. She faces demands for her obedience and appeals to her Humanity. She gingerly picks her way through her first nights among the Kindred, hoping to avoid enlisting unintentionally an elder's pet cause.

Precisely who are these powerful, aged Kindred who tempt her? How can they be so equally at home within both the city's darkened alleys and its brilliantly lit salons? Why do they seek her participation in their schemes when they could as easily slay her, or bend her will to their own with their centuries-old power? Why should such as they care one whit for the alliance of one so young and seemingly helpless as she? "They" are the elders, the Kindred who have withstood the test of time to survive beyond their neonate years and their ancilla decades to greet the centuries anew each night.

Playing an Elder

The exact point at which a vampire gains the designation of "elder" is not clear. Most Kindred agree that when a vampire manages to survive at least several centuries, she may begin using the title "elder" with some justification. The longevity requirement varies immensely around the world. To become an elder in Europe, for example, requires centuries more than it would in the New World. Despite these chronological disparities, elders are generally between 200 and 1,000 years old, give or take a century, and they are by and large Kindred of at least the eighth generation. What makes such characters so attractive to **Mind's Eye Theatre** players?

The Joy of Elders

Shall not the judge of all the earth do right?
— Genesis 18: 25

Elder characters are, by their very nature, more powerful than the average neonate or ancilla character. The elder's amassed strength is due largely to the fact that she has lived for so much longer than her younger cousins, gaining access over time to a greater number and wider range of Abilities, Influences and Disciplines. She gains a decided advantage in many situations, which many players can find appealing. Consider the practical advantages of an elder character:

— The elder's Blood Pool is greater than that of younger vampires, for she has learned over the centuries the means to extract the very last iota of supernatural energy from the vitae she consumes.

— An elder has honed her Attributes so that her limitations exceed those of most non-elder characters. For example, an elder may call upon a deeper reserve of Willpower, enabling her to compel or resist compulsion more readily than younger characters. These physical characteristics, in addition to age, are a large part of the reason why elders are usually treated with some modicum of respect. After all, it doesn't pay to mouth off to one who could leave your bones in splinters or wipe your mind clean like a slate.

— This enhanced reputation and respect often translates into actual status. Elders are, with few exceptions, influential figures in Kindred society, holding ranks as princes and primogen or bishops and paladins. Whatever their allegiance — Camarilla, Sabbat, or anarch — elders frequently occupy positions of authority, and are loath to surrender them to ambitious childer. To reinforce this pecking order, younger vampires are taught by their own sires and elders to heed the older members of their respective clan and sect and maintain a healthy respect for those elders of other clans as well.

Laws of Elysium

Playing an elder Kindred enables you to contribute a new element to your **Mind's Eye Theatre** game. An elder character has the potential to add a significant layer of depth to an existing chronicle. Your Storyteller may thrust you into the thick of any number of pre-existing conflicts, or she may use your character to introduce a new subplot or theme. An elder's impact on a story is almost immediately noticeable. For example, an elder automatically becomes a focal point for a variety of plots and subplots, simply due to her age and status. When younger Kindred are faced with puzzles, problems and mysteries, they often turn to their elders for direction. Your reaction to such pleas will determine the extent to which you become involved in these plots.

Later you may recognize that your character influences the game in more subtle ways. Let's say a current storyline includes an anarch pack lurking on the fringes of the city's vampire society. Then your character arrives. The anarchs will certainly want to know more about any elder who shows up in their city, and any elder would want to know more about potential diablerists. Your character may have to contend with anarch surveillance teams, or a test of her haven's defenses. She may even find herself squaring off against the anarchs later in the chronicle when the pack decides fully to announce its presence. Similarly, your character may unexpectedly tip the balance of power in favor of a particular clan. Are you playing a Toreador Artiste? Her arrival might spark a new wave of plans, both between clan members and any rival clans in the vicinity. From the first night your character enters the story, you should have no difficulty locating a plethora of conflicts and alliances. In fact, you may have to beat them away with a stick.

Harbingers of Doom

As far as we can discern, the sole purpose of human existence is to kindle a light of meaning in the darkness of mere being.

— Carl Jung, *Memories, Dreams, Reflections*

Power, even fictional power, is a drug, and there's no denying it is its own high. However, it is vital to recognize the equally indisputable fact that a proliferation of very powerful characters, or even one moderately powerful character played in an irresponsible fashion, can spell disaster for any chronicle. Great power requires great responsibility, even in a make-believe setting. It is far easier to destroy a chronicle than to create one, particularly within the live-action roleplaying paradigm. Your character can be the proverbial double-edged sword unless you are prepared to approach the task with some measure of responsibility and respect.

Playing an Elder

Responsible Roleplaying

Do not harbor sinister designs
— Miyamoto Musashi, The Book of Five Rings

Just as a rock thrown into the center of a pond causes ripples which eventually reach to the water's edge, so elders cause ripples on numerous levels. Recognize that your own character could have a similar effect on the game. Examine your character's abilities and powers in relation to the other characters in the game. Does your Ventrue possess *Presence* far beyond that attained by the majority of other Ventrue characters around him? Is your Tzimisce paladin the epitome of nocturnal horror, while your fellow packmates might be hard-pressed to intimidate a Toreador fledgling? If you recognize a disparity of this nature between your own character and those around you, you have an obligation not to ride roughshod simply because it is within your ability to do so. Rather, you should become one of the stewards of the story, helping to guide its ebb and flow in the most enjoyable directions.

The Masquerade is a cooperative storytelling experience. Each participant — player, Narrator, Storyteller — contributes in her own manner to the overall success of the story. The game depends entirely on the interactions between the various characters, and it is vital that you recognize that *all* the participants want to enjoy the experience as much as you do. Beating other characters into torpor each game session may be fun for you, but it's rarely enjoyable for the players on the receiving end. Violent acts that drastically affect other characters should occur within the context of the story itself, not as a method of dealing with other characters just because you can. It's one thing to discipline a neonate who thought she could mouth off to an elder, but entirely another to pick fights so you can show off your elder's Traits.

Creating an Elder Character

Working With Your Storyteller

Elder characters have the wherewithal to guide the game — indeed, they can (sometimes unintentionally) set the story's tone and pacing for an entire night, or even for the duration of a chronicle. Therefore, it is vital that you and the Storyteller be on the same page when you start creating the character. Set aside some time for you and the Storyteller to discuss your character's place in the story, and consider how your concept will fit into the existing framework. What might appear to be a perfect fit to you may actually be to the story's

detriment. The character may simply not mesh with the storyline, or it may prove disruptive and inappropriate for story-related reasons that the Storyteller cannot reveal to you. The better the Storyteller understands your character's powers, plans and background, the better she will be able to plan your character's involvement in the story.

Sometimes, you and your Storyteller may disagree on which characters are suited to the story. In such cases, trust your Storyteller. Be understanding and flexible; she's telling you this for a reason. If the Storyteller requests that you consider a different character, ask about character concepts and types which she believes will work with the story.

Elder Perspectives

The multiplying villainies of nature
  Do swarm upon him.
—William Shakespeare, Macbeth

Elder vampires do not spring into being overnight. Any character who is older than most countries usually sports a rich and colorful personal history. Consider your character's place in the history of the world and its vampire denizens — where has she been? What has she done? Where is she going? Thinking as a character who enjoys a potentially limitless lifespan is an exercise in advanced roleplaying, and one that you shouldn't skimp on.

Begin by thinking about your own life in comparison to the world events which have occurred during your lifetime. Do you remember the outbreak of World War II, the Cuban Missile Crisis, the assassination of President Kennedy, the Vietnam War, Watergate, U.S. hostages in Iran, the fall of the Berlin Wall or the Gulf War? Do you remember how you reacted to these events when you first read or learned about them? Did you understand then as well as you do now the effects these situations would have upon the world as you know it?

Next, try to think about some of the major events of this century that you do not remember as circumstances in your life. Take World War I, or the Jazz Era. What about the American stock market crash and the Great Depression? The more distant we become from events the less likely we are to recall their details. To gain a sense of their impact and place in history, we turn to books, films, plays and essays rather than to our own memories.

The same cannot be said for your elder vampire. She has existed for centuries, observing the affairs of the mortal world pass before her eyes as an endless parade of names, dates and headlines. How did she

Playing an Elder

react to these events? Did some of them affect her in material ways? Was she even aware of them as they transpired? Consider the events of your own life and your own perspective of time, and then magnify that same sensation 10 or 100 times. This marks the vast gulf in perspective and experience which yawns between the younger and older Kindred. Whereas neonates and ancillae may have observed several decades, or even an entire century, their sense of historical scope is dwarfed by that of the elders.

Instilling your character with some of this unique perspective is challenging but worth the effort, and makes interaction with you more interesting for the other players. If you take the time to perform some elementary historical research on the years during which your elder has lived, you will be able to give a much more convincing performance when your character discourses with other vampires, ghouls and mortals. Was your Gangrel sheriff present when Robert Bruce's troops fell at Bannockburn? Did your Lasombra bishop play a role in the Spanish *Reconquista*? Perhaps your Tremere insinuated himself among the mediums of the Age of Spiritualism, or maybe your Malkavian wrung her hands with glee when Nellie Bly exposed the horrific practices of 19th-century insane asylums.

Your character will gain a new depth and believability when your knowledge of past epochs manifests itself through roleplaying. Consider choosing one or two particular historical events which your character witnessed and research them more thoroughly. Think of sensory details for these stories, memories not only of sights, but also sounds (the screams of wounded horses), smells (the bay leaves and incense burned for the Oracle at Delphi), tastes (the blood of a drunken French courtier) and touches (the silk dressing gown you wore when you read the latest Sherlock Holmes mystery to relax).

Elder Motivations

Ah, that Deceit should steal such gentle shape
And with a virtuous vizor hide deep Vice!
—William Shakespeare, *Richard III*

What keeps you going? What are you here to accomplish? Elder characters require strong motives and desires to be believable. This is not to say that your character's motivation must be transparent — indeed, your character's desires and goals should remain concealed until such time as you choose to reveal them. Many (if not most) of your character's actions will be dictated by her core motivations, and

Laws of Elysium

flimsy motives will make even the best concept look unrealistic. After creating the bare bones of your character, turn your attention to developing and defining those impulses which will govern your character's interactions through the story.

• **Security** —Though you embody vast powers and knowledge, you are by no means omnipotent or invulnerable; you will often find yourself caught between the hammer and the anvil. To one side are the Methuselahs, and perhaps the mysterious and terrifying Antediluvians. Elders are the pawns of choice for both groups in their eternal Jyhad. Those elders who are not already controlled by Methuselahs or Antediluvians continually struggle to avoid the same fate. Whenever you meet another elder, you must consider who might have their fingers on his strings. To the other side wait the energetic younger Kindred, ever ready to usurp their elders' authority and embarrass them by wrecking the most carefully laid plans. Worse than this, however, is the terrifying prospect of the fledglings who may hunt you for the purpose of claiming your power as their own. Small wonder, then, that many elders spend their nights motivated by a desire to ensure their own safety amid the dangers and upheavals which surround them.

• **Status**—Elders, whether Sabbat paladins or Camarilla primogen, enjoy a certain elevated status among their chosen societies. Within the Camarilla, status is essential for the security and continued functioning of the sect, and is thus of paramount importance to many Kindred. Indeed, for some elders status and its reward are all that truly matters to them. Elders crave the deference of the power-hungry ancillae, the reverence of the neonates and the respect of their peers. Many go to great lengths in pursuit of additional status, and even greater lengths to maintain that which they already possess, buying and trading Status Traits as if they were the most precious commodities on Earth. Rival elders continually seek to diminish each other's status, and may even wage subtle wars with status as the spoils of victory.

Status loses none of its importance in the Sabbat, although it is based on characteristics quite different from those found in its rival sect. Likewise, status among Sabbat Kindred may often be utilized for other, unexpected purposes. Because status within the Sabbat is so easily gained and lost, more than a few Sabbat elders are continually conscious of their current status and eagerly pursue more as a means of controlling younger vampires and avoiding time-wasting challenges to their authority.

Playing an Elder

- **Political Power** — It has been observed that power is a drug, that its taste is sweeter even than the most quenching blood. Elders are as accustomed to holding positions of temporal power as they are to gaining status, but for some the pursuit of the former is far more exhilarating and meaningful than chasing the latter (some may perceive power and status to be one and the same, but it is quite possible to have one without the other). Once an elder painstakingly claws her way up the ladder of Kindred society to reach the upper echelons, she will be more than reluctant to relinquish her success to the vampires occupying the rungs below. In fact, she will fight with all the viciousness she can command to maintain her place, for power allows a vampire to gain control over her immediate surroundings. This need to control their environment burns in the minds of many elders, motivating them to engage in mind-bending intrigues to achieve or maintain their authority.

  Power is a dangerous goal, however, for you will find it necessary to utilize questionable means to attain it. Advancing your personal agenda may require blackmail, threats, bribes and other tools of subversion. Politics are, by their very nature, a public pursuit; it can become difficult to conceal your machinations from prying eyes. If you begin to reach your goal, this draws rivals and others bent on usurping your hard-won authority. Conflicts with rivals and equally power-hungry ancillae intent on claiming the same prize make this motivation challenging to play, although many who seek power say that such challenges merely make the goal all the more satisfying once it is attained.

- **Golconda** — While the elders who actively seek this fabled state of inner equilibrium are rare, such Kindred do exist. The outward actions and appearances of an elder who navigates the uncertain waters that lead to atonement may not appear any different from those of the elder motivated by more common goals. She strives to gain a tangible measure of mastery over the Beast, to deny its continual demands in order to gain some degree of acceptance of her own vampiric nature. This motivation is highly personal, and manifests itself in a somewhat more subtle fashion than others, for it is only through interactions with others of her own kind that the character understands herself enough to satisfy the rigorous demands of this path.

  An interesting variation on this motivation is the elder who has already attained Golconda and who wishes to share the gift with his fellow Kindred. Such a motivation, while laudable, is fraught with hardship and peril, for he is once again plunged into the thick of the

horror from which he recoiled. In demonstrating his sincerity, he may well find himself tempted by the very acts and passions which first set him on this path. If he is to convince anyone else of the possibility of redemption, though, he must not only face his inner demons but prevail against them again.

• **Return to Yesteryear** — The selfsame conditions that bring about elders' desire to exert excessive control may manifest themselves in the wish to return to the familiar customs and habits of long-dead ages. Some examples include the Brujah elder who gives herself completely over to her dream of transforming her chosen domain into the reincarnation of ancient Carthage, or the Tzimisce whose wish is to rule once again a kingdom as an omnipotent warlord as he did in the Carpathians three centuries past. Yearning to recreate the imagined glories of the past may motivate the elder to proclaim her goals publicly and recruit followers who listen to her tales of a better time. The elder may also try to manipulate events around her to reflect the world she enjoyed in nights gone by.

• **Revenge** — Unusual indeed is the elder who has not wronged and been wronged by another of her kind during her eternal existence. The events that light and fan the fires of vengeance are legion, and in many cases your search for retribution may seem right in your eyes. Perhaps a rival elder's plan to embarrass you in front of her peers cost you the seat on a primogen council, or another Kindred wounded you and left you for dead. Maybe a pack of anarchs slew your sire or childe, or your packmates betrayed you rather than risk capture when a Sabbat raid went awry. You should have no difficulty creating an appropriately gruesome or horrific deed that left a memory gnawing at your gut every night of your unlife. Forever is a long time to nurse a grudge, and the desire for vengeance can be so strong that it will not do simply to murder the object of your hatred once you find him. It is often far more satisfying to plan an elaborate act of revenge in which your target is fully aware of his humiliation and its source.

• **Romance** — While it is true that many elders' emotions have waned over the long night, it is still possible for an elder to feel the dizzying intoxication of passion for another Kindred, or even for a favored ghoul or mortal. The sudden blossoming of such love could be a complete surprise to your elder, and he may struggle against it, trying to deny the upheaval of his plans and his carefully ordered existence. Depending on your selected Nature and Demeanor, the pursuit of a romantic goal can manifest itself in any number of ways. Perhaps you

Playing an Elder

become infatuated with a mortal from among your many Influences who reminds you of a past lover. It may be that you and another character in the chronicle once shared a passion which has cooled over the centuries, and which you now wish to rekindle. Unrequited love can be among the most powerful of romantic motivations — attempting to prove your worth to a lover who spurns or ignores you is an intriguing alternative to the usual romantic entanglements. What if the lover in question is a younger Kindred or mortal trying desperately to win your favor? Because of the power differences between elders and other characters, and because of the very nature of live-action roleplay, be certain to establish the bounds of the romantic plotline with the player(s) who are participating in it with you.

• **Insanity** — The crushing weight of the years, the growing isolation from the mortal world, the unending attacks on your power, the slow retreat from your own humanity — these elements of life as an elder can drive you into the arms of insanity as surely as the most violent or sudden trauma. Maybe your character acquired several Beast Traits or Derangements which cause her to act in an increasingly unpredictable and dangerous manner. Perhaps she simply can't cope with immortality any longer and harbors a secret wish for her own destruction.

Note: Insanity does not give you license to act without thinking. While your actions may appear to observers to be completely random, irrational or inexplicable, make certain that your madness has method in it. Otherwise it becomes a parody of itself, a disjointed series of nonsensical ravings or wildly inappropriate scenes that diminish the game's enjoyment for everyone. An insane person — particularly an insane elder — operates according to an established internal logic. While your motivations will not be understood by those around you, they should be consistent with the altered point of view brought on by your madness.

Effective Roleplaying

The fire which seems out often sleeps beneath the cinders.
— Pierre Coneille

Your role as an elder has many facets. Your character embodies the ancient authority older Kindred wield over the younger, and therefore will be asked (or pressured) to participate in the ongoing interactions between the various strata of vampire society. It is important to understand how your character will likely relate to the various factions which also inhabit the night.

Puttin' On the Ritz

Silk or leather? Etruscan or Mod? Having seen (and occasionally played) the fashion game, most elders are jaded to the notion of clothes and fashion. As long as it covers the body, many couldn't care less what they're actually wearing. In the case of some (such as the Lasombra), the matter of appearance is immensely important, particularly when one requires assistance in dressing.

One part of LARPing that is always uppermost in many players' minds is costuming and looking the part. Everyone wants to look his best, and elders (and their players) are no different. Some relish the opportunity to wear their favorite vintage and step out in style. Others…need a little help. When the Brujah neonates are outshining your elders on a regular basis, or the Tremere elder's player arrives in a nylon cape fresh from the package and announces that he's in costume, it's time to take a hand in things. Dressing for the part need not be an exercise in frustration. With a little preparation and thought, the elders can be the belles of the ball as they deservedly should be.

Start by considering your elder's age. When was she Embraced? How long has she lived? What time periods did she actually experience? What was she doing? If she was in torpor for most of the 18th century, it doesn't make sense to consider Watteau gowns for her wardrobe. If, however, some of her happiest nights were spent as a silent film star during the '20s, then perhaps dropped-waist dresses or slinky evening gowns are an avenue worth exploring. Likewise, if she spent most of the "Gay '90s" engaged in warfare with another elder, then she may associate wearing such clothes with her hated nemisis.

If you want ideas about the sorts of things your character might have worn, head to the library and check out books of fashion and period portraits, or watch historical movies. You don't need to know all the terms; just look at the styles and see what appeals to you. You might have considered Victorian for your elder, but you're not ready to start corseting. On the other hand, the soft lines of the gowns of the 1930s, complete with gloves and a little hat, are appealing and more comfortable-looking. Your Ventrue elder was active in London, then, a society maven — and like that, you have a potential idea for something much different from the usual ruck and run of Victorian and 18th century fashions.

Playing an Elder

Obviously, the Masquerade should be a consideration. Let's say your Brujah elder was Embraced during the era of Socrates and Plato, and finds Greek robes to be the most comfortable thing he's ever worn in the past 2000-plus years. A man wandering down the streets at night wearing a chiton and sandals is bound to attract attention, some of which will certainly be undesirable. And how many times would *you* want to be asked if you're in a play? You might want to save the robes for wearing around the haven. If you're determined to have something Greek on your elder's person, consider something small, like a ring with a Grecian key design or a tie showing decorations from an urn.

They say that clothes make the man, and certainly clothes carry connotations about your character, however unintentional. Someone who refuses to put on modern dress at all may find himself viewed as a relic, and a doddering one at that, pining for the "good old days." In fact, most younger Kindred expect elders to look like antiques, partly for identifying plumage. A Ventrue elder never seen in a modern suit will be unlikely to garner respect, while a Brujah elder who still insists on dressing like an Iconoclast may find it difficult to be taken seriously by his elder peers. Likewise, an elder who tries too hard to outshine others will be dismissed as a fool, since she should be above that sort of thing (or at least it shouldn't be overt). In response to this perception, however, some elders have trusted younger childer or mortal assistants who advise them on the changes in clothing and help them look a little less outdated.

Vintage clothing stores should be the first stop of anyone searching for an elder's garb. A good piece, cared for well, will last you through many evenings of intrigue. Even small accessories, like gloves, handkerchiefs, calling card cases and the like can bring an outfit (and character) to life. For snappy modern dressing, check out resale shops in your area, particularly those that advertise "gently used" garments. Many times, these places carry outfits barely out of season, and certainly not out of style.

If you have friends who sew and construct costumes, consider offering yourself as a guinea pig. Couture offers them the chance to experiment with fabrics and styles, and when it's done, you have an outfit that's completely different from anything else that will show up at Elysium. It can also provide some great plot threads about where your character gets her clothes done.

Maintaining the Status Quo

Elders have a vested interest in maintaining the status quo, whatever the circumstances of their individual situations may be. It would be absurd to think that you would allow your hard-won status, power and authority to be snatched from your hands by overeager, undeserving upstarts of weaker generations. No prince casually surrenders the throne to an ambitious ancilla; no elder willingly turns over her primogen seat to an impetuous fledgling. This is the paradox of Kindred existence — the constant ambition of the neonates and ancillae to achieve the same rewards as the elders, juxtaposed with the elders' desperate measures to thwart these attempts at any cost.

You will probably find it beneficial to your elder existence to resist sudden or drastic change in the status quo, unless such nontraditional behavior clearly benefits your position. Greet sweeping proposals for social reform as but one step removed from anarchy. React to suggested business improvements with barely concealed disinterest, promising to review the plans as soon as your busy schedule permits. Stamp out the anarch threat wherever and whenever it may be found, for the dissatisfied grumblings of youth soon turn to the scorching flame of rebellion. Above all, instill in the younger, less experienced Kindred a mortal fear of the enemy, whether it be Camarilla or Sabbat. Point out that this hated foe's victory would be all but assured if the elders were to fail in their unceasing vigilance, and that the city would have fallen for certain were it not for your own tireless efforts against the adversary.

Dealing with Kindred Society

Some players view elder characters simply as a means of crushing all who cross their paths during a game. They leave a trail of mangled characters behind them, and turn even more viciously on any character who dares admonish them. Such a player should expect to be shunned by the rest, or even expelled from the chronicle, and deservedly so. While violence is part and parcel of the World of Darkness, habitually behaving in this manner simply to gain attention or to disrupt the game shows a lack of the maturity necssary for playing a powerful character. Elevating the story above the pitfalls of mindless violence is the equal responsibility of every player, but particularly those who portray elders, since they have the capacity to inflict the most damage with the least amount of effort.

Playing an Elder

As an elder, you should be willing to help guide the game in the direction that is most entertaining for everyone, not just yourself. Your Storyteller trusts you with the potential to help make or break the game, and in a way trusts you with a measure of responsibility for the game. This is not to say that you must perpetually sacrifice your own enjoyment, but rather that you should be equally aware of your fellow players' needs alongside your own.

How, then, should you deal with those Kindred who lack your age and capabilities? What do you say to the neonate who insults you at the prince's court, or do to the ancilla who ruins plans that took years to lay? Wise elders master their immediate impulse to destroy the offender, and instead embark upon a time-honored campaign for the loyalties, hearts and minds of their detractors and supporters alike.

Most chronicles will feature some degree of stratification between character power levels. A few characters will probably be elders, and thus relatively more powerful in terms of resources and capabilities. The majority of characters will probably be ancillae and neonates, the rank and file of the Kindred world. In this type of game, successful elder characters work to improve their individual power bases, without calling undue attention to themselves. You did not survive to become an elder, after all, by stepping boldly to the front every time danger threatened and volunteers were requested. You, as an elder, should not *want* to pursue every plot thread or story line that comes your way. Instead, encourage your more "youthful" allies, associates and subordinates to investigate the strange occurrences, unusual circumstances and mysterious happenings while you remain "behind the lines" to direct the action.

Interacting with Neonates

Some elders make the mistake of viewing neonates as little more than flunkies, beasts of burden, slaves or scapegoats. These elders, secure in the belief that their elevated status will protect them from reprisal from the weaker strata of vampire society, don't feel they need to bother with neonates. Nothing could be further from the truth. A single neonate equipped with knowledge and training is worth twice the value of the most loyal ghoul retainer or mortal servant. Several neonates who decide to combine forces are sometimes quite capable of taking down a single elder.

Neonates who reject the status quo are exceedingly dangerous — call attention to the threat they represent at every opportunity.

Laws of Elysium

Rebellious Camarilla neonates sometimes flee the sect and form anarch packs, dedicated to insurrection and destruction of the elders' precious status quo. Worse, they may be recruited by the Sabbat and turned into weapons pointed directly at the Camarilla's heart. Sabbat neonates who break free of their elders' control are no longer useful tools to be used against the hated Camarilla. At best they wander without direction; at worst they might join the enemy. For these reasons it is vital that you, as a prudent elder, treat neonates not as chattel but as a valuable resource. Unless you want them to start preaching against the established order — and against you as its defender — consider them as the building blocks of your own power base.

Befriending neonates is an excellent in-game method of simultaneously fostering character interaction and supporting elder involvement in the story. You will find it more than worth your investment in time and energy to recruit a network of less powerful characters who will do your bidding (voluntarily or otherwise), leaving you free to pursue more genteel diversions. If you are even marginally successful in recruiting associates and helpers across clan lines, so much the better, for your power base will be that much more enhanced.

Once established, your neonate support system is not necessarily secure. You will almost certainly find yourself competing with other elders, and sometimes ancillae, for control of this precious resource. Rival Kindred are quite capable of utilizing methods similar to those you initially employed to gain the neonates' assistance. Do you regularly use shouted threats and beatings to instill fear and respect in your neonate followers? You can be certain that the other elders of the city know about it, and are whispering into the neonate's ear when you're out of earshot. Watch for elder manipulators who attempt to sow dissent within the ranks of your helpers and associates. If you fail to guard your young followers jealously against poachers, defections will become commonplace. Consider the system of rewards and punishments you use to retain neonate loyalty. Too much or too little of either one erodes your power base as surely as a rival's blandishments.

Neonates perform a plethora of vital functions for their elders. They make effective bodyguards when you travel, or guard your haven while you attend to business. Neonates can also be your eyes and ears when you need to be in two places at once. A primogen

Playing an Elder

meeting may command the bulk of your attention on a given night, but your young spies can keep tabs on the Gangrel who started sniffing around your newly constructed chemical plant, reporting to you later on her movements and conversations.

Perhaps most importantly, neonates are capable of understanding the modern world more readily than you are. Face it, you are the product of a bygone era, and in spite of your age and power, you may need assistance in dealing with modern technology and customs. Computer systems, for example, are sufficiently difficult for contemporary mortals to understand and utilize effectively. To a vampire whose last intimate contact with technology was with the telegraph, flintlock rifle or aqueduct, such machines may prove incomprehensible. Neonates whose mortal lives were contemporary with these devices can be invaluable for helping you harness this technology for your own benefit. Those with computer expertise can help you decimate a rival's economic empire, search for information or spread rumors and innuendo throughout an entirely new medium.

Interacting with Ancillae

This "middle class" within vampire society is at once indispensably useful and exceedingly dangerous. If the ancillae could be bothered to set aside their own selfish pursuits and internecine squabbling, they would be a force to be reckoned with, one which could conceivably challenge the elders' iron grip on the night. Many elders live in fear of this potential usurpation, and maintain constant vigilance against it. Dealing with ancillae can prove costly if you misjudge or anger them. At the same time, you cannot afford to show unnecessary weakness or incompetence, lest you inspire the ancillae to unseat you.

If the neonates are the foundation of your power base, then the ancillae are the mortar which holds the stones together. A capable ancilla can perform many useful functions, such as acting as a mediator between you and the neonates you wish to recruit to your side, or as a troubleshooter to alert you when your plans are going astray. Ancillae also make excellent advisors and lieutenants, administering your holdings or businesses on your behalf and informing you of important developments within your fields of interests.

You must beware your subordinates' ambitions, however. Make no mistake — the ancilla to whom you entrust your most secret

plans may well be plotting to betray you and assume your place. You need to determine the correct balance between reward and punishment to keep the ancillae in line and on your side. If you reward them with too much too often, they will come to expect your gratitude even when they haven't earned it. If you reward them with too little or too seldom, they will grow resentful at your ingratitude and be easy targets for rivals.

Establishing Alliances

How, then, can the neonates and ancillae be drawn as moths to your flame?

• Goodwill — Few tactics surpass good manners in impressing your associates. Simply behaving courteously toward the younger generations can often establish you as an elder who values them and their contributions. If your Nature and Demeanor permit, try praising the young Ventrue who greets you in a respectful manner, or complimenting the Toreador ingenue on her new frock. Such small gestures cost you very little, and can reap an impressive return in your future dealings with the young ones. Neonates and ancillae whom you take care to compliment may find your later overtures of alliance more believable and palatable. If you are fortunate, your evident goodwill may even induce a younger Kindred to reject a request made by one of your rivals to do you harm. It's sometimes equally useful to point out the discourtesy shown by other, less sensitive elders to the younger Kindred. If a situation should occur wherein both you or the unmannered elder both desire the neonate's services, whom do you think the young vampire will be more likely to consider? Occasional small gifts of information, advice, constructive criticism and perhaps even Status can also do wonders to set you apart from the elders who believe that the best way to treat neonates and ancillae is with the tip of their boot.

• Blackmail — Where goodwill sometimes fails, blackmail may sometimes succeed. Perhaps a headstrong childe rebuffed your friendly overtures? No matter — all Kindred hide secrets, and few wish their weak spots revealed. Perhaps the Gangrel's sire didn't abandon her after all, but rather fell victim to his progeny's appetites? Perhaps the Ventrue whip would not care to have his rather obscure feeding habits bandied about the prince's court for the amusement of others? Threats of exposure are best when made subtly, but you must bait this hook well — if your price for silence is too high, you may well become

Playing an Elder

the next target of your "victim." Moreover, make certain that what you ask is within your target's ability to give. You cannot obtain a vast fortune from an impoverished childe, after all.

• **Threats** — Elders who are skilled in making threats find that implied consequences are better than those stated explicitly. Blatant warnings of imminent harm seldom do more than earn your target's temporary cooperation, followed by her long-term enmity. Most threats are more effective in the short term, and often the same threat does not work twice. There are some excellent examples of long-term threats, however, such as blackmail (see above) or warnings of serious injury to those beloved by your target. Neonates may respond more readily than ancillae to threats of physical violence, although sometimes just the hint of inconvenience can be sufficient to forge a brief alliance. Beware whom you threaten, however, as you will not be the only elder practicing such techniques. Threatening ancillae or neonates whom you know to be strongly supported by other elders is an invitation to disaster. Choose both your threat and threatened with care.

• **Blood Bond** — Be wary of using the Blood Bond indiscriminately, particularly on those Kindred who are not your own progeny. If you try to create an army of Blood Bound servitors, other elders in the vicinity will almost certainly try to prevent it, before it upsets the balance of power. They may even decide to unite against you, which could prove disastrous. If you choose to employ the Bond as a means of influencing a younger Kindred, consider keeping the attachment a secret. Your enemies may trust your Thrall more readily if they are unaware that you are her Regnant.

• **Lies** — No one ever said that you must always tell the truth when dealing with younger Kindred (indeed, some neonates and ancillae would claim that the reverse is usually true). The kind of response you can provoke with a judicious lie can be both surprising and gratifying. Perhaps a certain Brujah is burning for revenge on the unknown assassin who murdered his sire. Should you hint that you know, or can somehow determine, the killer's identity, you may earn the childe's services. Is your packmate willing to do anything to please the pack leader? Consider letting it "slip" that you know the way to win her approval, and will gladly reveal it in exchange for a small favor. If your falsehood is exposed, discovered by your target or revealed by a rival, it's best to conceal it with more lies in order to avoid the consequences of revealing the truth.

Laws of Elysium

Interacting with Elders

Some of the most dynamic moments in any chronicle arise from the interactions between elders. These vampiric peers circle one another like wary gladiators, seeking their opponent's weak spots while striving not to reveal any of their own. Elders do assist one another, but such aid almost always carries a price which must be paid in full before or immediately after services are rendered. Thus the games of one-upmanship are played out against the backdrop of elder interaction, with each player jockeying to place herself in a position to bestow favors and demand the appropriate gratitude in return.

It's a good idea to be respectful of other elders, at least in public. While it's sometimes difficult to conceal your contempt for a sneering rival or a member of an opposed clan, hurling insults rarely accomplishes anything beyond antagonizing the target of your scorn. Likewise, attacking other elders is almost always a bad idea. Would you really want to go toe-to-toe with someone as old and powerful as yourself? Unless you are purposefully trying to goad your fellow elder into a response, it is usually wisest to keep a civil tongue in your head.

Other elders can be your closest allies or your most dreaded enemies. They often want the same things you want, and are as well-versed as you in the art of obtaining what they wish. They are in competition with you for the scarce resources of the World of Darkness, such as the services of neonates and ancillae. They will strive to acquire the same advantages you desire, not least among them mortal vessels and Influence, and it is from this competition that many of the fiercest and most long-standing elder feuds are created. Tread lightly among your fellow ancients.

Avoiding Unnecessary Violence

Consider a typical night at the prince's court. You prepare hours in advance, dressing in your most expensive finery, choosing just the right tie to win approving glances from the Harpies, and taking the time to make certain your appearance is as perfect as money can buy. You are confident that your plan to cement an alliance with the Toreador elder will reach fruition this evening. You arrive in your new luxury car, your driver smart and efficient, and make your grand entrance through the wide mahogany doors into the vast reception hall…only to collide with

Playing an Elder

another Kindred carrying a pair of goblets overflowing with vitae, which now forms indelible stains on your clothing for all to see. Because you are an elder no one laughs openly, but you can hear the undercurrent of amusement pass through the gathering like an electric shock. Taking your eyes from your ruined clothing, you gaze upon the face of your destroyer, a newly Embraced neonate of the Brujah clan. Rage takes root in your heart and pulsates quickly to the roof of your mouth, flame-hot as the Beast screams in your mind that you must be allowed the sight of this childe's blood on your hands. The neonate stares in mute horror at your clothes, then at the expression of white-hot anger on your face. Your eyes flick momentarily to the gathered crowd, and you see the Toreador elder smiling wryly as she shakes her head at your misfortune, then turns to whisper into the ear of one of the Harpies....

What Do You Do Now?

A — Kill the offending Brujah neonate without mercy or hesitation! You are an elder, after all, and are entitled to respect from whelps like him. The insult is unforgivable, and may well have been planned, a calculated "accident" to embarrass you and forestall your alliance with the Toreador. A swift death for this childe will serve as an object lesson for any other Kindred who seeks to make you play the fool!

B — Reprimand the unwise childe with a scathing, public tongue-lashing, then spend the next three months plotting his grisly death. Your vengeance will be delicious, no less than the complete dismemberment of this upstart pup, who will only at the moment of his Final Death suddenly recognize you as the engineer of his demise. You can savor his death screams already!

C — Begin a campaign to glean as many reparations as possible from the Brujah clan in payment for this unfortunate accident. You will play the proud but injured party and demand that the Brujah primogen punish the neonate for this transgression, but will recommend leniency — after all, you want the childe alive so that his fear of your eventual reprisal will haunt him each morning when he sleeps. You could kill him any time, but making his life miserable with anxiety is far more satisfying. What's more, you'll use this encounter as proof for the Toreador elder that the Brujah are too uncivilized to stand in the way of your alliance.

If you answered:

A — Please report to the nearest medical facility for your lobotomy. It's better this way, honest.

Laws of Elysium

B — Your sense of drama does you credit, but if you react to all inconveniences in this matter, your passions will eventually be your undoing.

C — Congratulations! You are among the superior elders! You have realized that violence should be applied in the game like a surgical instrument — with precision and skillful direction, and certainly not as a first resort.

This example is not meant to suggest that it is never appropriate for an elder to use violence against a neonate or an ancilla. There may be circumstances in which such an outcome is unavoidable, and may even support the story. Death should always remain a very real threat in the game, otherwise there is little to prevent characters from running completely amuck. In many cases, however, you may find it more effective to conserve your energy, saving your strength in preparation for combating more deadly foes, such as other elders.

Rash acts of murder often lead to unpleasant consequences. If your victim was prominent among her clan, for example, her death may lead to interclan war. Such outcomes are undesirable, for they often derail an entire chronicle and require drastic manhandling from the Storyteller to put the story back on track. Engaging in combat too frequently also attracts unwanted attention from the prince, his sheriff and sometimes the archons, a fate most wise elders avoid. Elders who cannot control their violent impulses may be judged a danger to the Traditions, giving a prince the necessary excuse to call a Blood Hunt or request assistance from a Justicar. Frequent, overt violence can also lead to inadvertent breaches of the Masquerade, which no Kindred can afford to take lightly. Habitually violent Kindred often find themselves ostracized from Kindred society, and may find it difficult to retain their status and influence. If you are the type of player who engages in numerous Physical Challenges for the sheer enjoyment of beating up on other characters, it might be best if you found another pastime before any of these unfortunate occurrences befall your character.

It is worth bearing in mind that the elders are more acutely aware of the dangers of violating the First Tradition than some of their young cousins. Some elders remember the nights of terror dominated by the Inquisition, when the mortal world turned against them and dragged so many of them screaming into the sunlight or burned them beside heretics and elderly widows in the witch-fires. These memories, and the dread of such circumstances once again coming to pass, give many

Playing an Elder

elders a healthy aversion to rash brutality. Too much impulsive violence escalates into pitched battles which in turn threaten or even violate the Masquerade, and for this reason many elders use violent means only as a last resort.

There are effective, nonlethal solutions to almost any situation which might arise over the course of a chronicle, and most of these reprisals fully support the volatile, dangerous nature of the World of Darkness. Acts of vengeance which allow your victim to survive are often preferable to the more final variety for one simple reason — the object of your revenge remains alive for future retribution and abuse. Why destroy the Toreador who seduced your favorite ghoul when you could inflict a humbling, nonlethal lesson on her, leaving her around for more reprisals in the nights to come? Choosing to end all conflicts by killing one's enemies is shortsighted, and a hallmark of the problem player.

Should you find yourself wronged, offended or slighted in some material way by another Kindred, you may wish to consider approaching the offender's sire or primogen and discussing the manner in which he could make reparations for your inconvenience. In some Camarilla-controlled cities, the primogen are at least somewhat accountable for the actions of their respective clans, and are frequently responsible for keeping their more "enthusiastic" brethren in line.

Be open to Prestation, and you may find yourself the recipient of a valuable boon in exchange for your willingness to overlook an unfortunate incident. This type of reparation is most common when the offense and apology are committed and made in public. Rather than destroying a rude neonate for insulting you before the primogen, consider instead the value of forgiving the offense in favor of exacting a promise of future aid from the whelp's embarrassed sire. Publicly forgive the rash act and accept the boon in private; you will appear magnanimous and genteel, rather than a vain and pompous bully. Don't be greedy — accept a Boon commensurate with the offense. It will make you look foolish to demand a Life Boon for overlooking a relatively minor transgression. If an expected offer of Prestation is not forthcoming, don't make an issue of it, but later in the evening you may want to make "casual" mention to the Harpy about the shocking lack of manners exhibited both by the neonate and her sire.

Sometimes a Kindred who has wronged you will be eager to make up for her actions in order to avert your wrath, but will be anxious to avoid any public acknowledgment. You are an elder, after all, and your displeasure cannot be taken lightly. By simply acting annoyed and perhaps angered with the transgressor, you may elicit the offer of something valuable to soothe your ruffled feathers — the loan of useful Influence, for example, or perhaps an offer to teach you a new Discipline. Some elders are not above accepting cash, information or other valuable commodities in return for not pressing a delicate matter.

How to Get the Most Out of Your Elder

I do not despair in the least of ultimate triumph. I repeat it with intense conviction.

— Emile Zola

You will soon discover that the game itself seldom makes it necessary to resort to something as blatant as outright violence to secure your desires. **The Masquerade** contains a number of subtle methods for gaining the upper hand through roleplaying, which is almost always the most satisfying means. Two of the most effective game components in facilitating the triumph of subtlety over violence are Influence and Prestation.

Influence: Mortal Allies

The elder who masters an Influence in her city or region gains an impressive resource on which to draw in her efforts to secure her station and thwart those who would usurp it. Elders may rule the night and hold sway over the activities of the Kindred, but the mortal world hums on unceasingly around them. While elders sleep, their mortal retainers and allies are alert and mobile, guarding their master's interests and carrying out her wishes. Mastery of an Influence can offer you a considerable advantage in your nightly business.

Your elder character may, at your Storyteller's discretion, begin the game with a number of Influence Traits in excess of the normal three most characters obtain at the time of their creation. If so, you must decide whether to concentrate on dominating just one or two areas of Influence, or to spread your Traits as widely as possible in order to obtain access to many different facets of mortal society. If your Ventrue elder begins the game with five Influence Traits, for example, you might decide to invest all five in the *Finance* Influence, in addition to the one free *Finance* Influence Trait all Ventrue gain at character creation, giving you six Traits of *Finance* Influence and

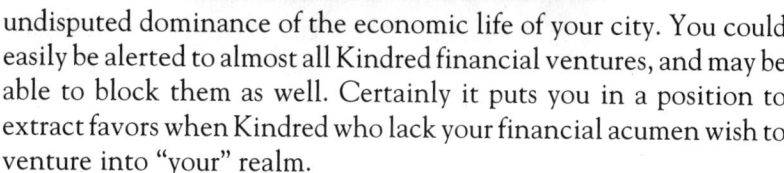

Playing an Elder

undisputed dominance of the economic life of your city. You could easily be alerted to almost all Kindred financial ventures, and may be able to block them as well. Certainly it puts you in a position to extract favors when Kindred who lack your financial acumen wish to venture into "your" realm.

You might, however, decide to assign three Influences Traits to the *Finance* Influence, two to *Bureaucracy* and one to *Industry*. You would then have a more diverse power base, making it less likely that any crippling blow to any single Influence under your sway would damage you permanently. Moreover, you gain information from a wider array of sources, and if you find it necessary to trade Influences with other Kindred, possessing a variety of Traits often makes such deals easier to complete. Ultimately, your own sense of your character's Nature and your interpretation of her motivations will determine how you choose to spread your Influences.

Influence Traits can be used to great effect within the scope of an ongoing chronicle. They are one of the most potent weapons in any vampire's arsenal, often far more sure and lethal than the claw or gun. If your Storyteller does not already have you reporting your monthly Influence activity, start indicating exactly what your Influences are working on between games. It is possible to inconvenience or even crush an enemy thoroughly through prolonged, concentrated use of Influences, and the end result can be far more satisfying than a crude bloodletting. The shrewd use and trading of Influences can gain you an enormous amount of prestige for your subtlety.

Control of the *Police* Influence, for example, can enable you to wreak havoc on your enemies. You can order their havens disturbed during daylight hours, or have their own Influences arrested and detained for questioning. The police can cordon off buildings and streets while you tend to your business undisturbed, and they can allow you to ensure that certain pieces of incriminating evidence collected from crime scenes simply vanish into the night air. Equally useful is the *Industry* Influence. Is your rival a shipping magnate who prides himself on his access to container ships? A prolonged strike among the longshoremen, dock laborers or even tugboat pilots can cripple his business and deprive him of income. Likewise, an artificial shortage of vital resources like ore or chemicals can make life miserable for those Kindred with manufacturing interests. Criminal harassment instigated through the *Underworld* Influence can make it nearly impossible for other

Kindred to do business, while the ability to seize control of City Hall via *Politics* can bring other vampires crawling to you when they need help in passing a city ordinance or dealing with bureaucratic red tape.

In addition to inflicting harm, your Influence Traits can be used to gather vital information which enables you to remain one step ahead of the rest of the pack. They may be utilized to lend support to your allies in time of need (in return for later favors, of course). Such categories as *Street*, *Health* and *University* can prove invaluable in finding out exactly what is happening in your local area, or in obtaining such valuable resources as vitae and cash when supplies are low. Wise selection of Influences can offer you a safe emergency haven when your plans go wrong, and easy access to vessels when other methods of hunting are not viable.

Prestation

The millennia-honored game of Prestation is one of your most potent means of safeguarding the ultimate success of your plans. It is no overstatement to say that learning to understand and appreciate Prestation fully may mean the difference between gaining authority among the Kindred and falling under the heel of your rivals.

The most basic lesson in Prestation is "Nobody gets nothing for free." Did you supply the sheriff with a tip on where she could apprehend the anarchs who have been smuggling guns into the city? Did you permit the prince's favorite childe safe passage through your network of sewers? Did you endanger your own safety by stepping in to protect the Toreador primogen from the Assamite's near-fatal blow? In all cases, you are within your rights to politely remind the other party that it is customary to return such favors in kind, and since you have no immediate need of a similar service, you would be pleased to accept a Boon as a token of appreciation. Remembering that every favor, however small, is probably worth something to somebody can help you build an impressive library of Boons. Even a collection of minor Boons bestowed upon you by Kindred of lesser station or age can be valuable, especially when you consider that they can be traded (exactly like Influences) to other Kindred in return for other favors and aid.

Prestation is a game of subtlety, however. Strive to avoid giving those in your debt the opportunity to repay you. A Boon

Playing an Elder

repaid is no longer of value. Not all Kindred will stand idly by while they owe you respect and debt by virtue of giving you a Boon, though — some Kindred may attempt to force the issue by arranging circumstances so that you will have little choice but to allow them to repay the debt. Others may even go so far as to attempt to remove the inconvenience the Boon represents by trying to place you in their debt, or even trying to eliminate the Boon by eliminating the one who holds it. Be certain to alert the Harpies, prince or other authority figures if a vampire in your debt reneges on or ignores a Boon rightfully owed to you. This kind of pressure can be nearly as effective in embarrassing or controlling your rivals as possession of the Boon itself.

Storytelling for Elders

Working with elder characters is a challenge. Plots and subplots can spin off in unexpected directions. One moment the plot is moving along and your players are enjoying themselves. In the next moment, the game's setting is in flames, the Masquerade is completely blown, and the natives are restless. The game is out of control, and it's up to you to get it back on track.

This chapter contains essential information for Storytellers who wish to run chronicles and independent stories involving elders. The techniques and pitfalls of the all-elder chronicle are discussed in depth. This chapter will also help you troubleshoot elder-created and elder-associated problems, and offers advice on repairing a derailed plot. Following this are ideas and methods for integrating elders into your regular chronicle. Finally, there is information on how to guide your players as their characters advance toward elder status, and the important issues which inevitably arise during this process.

The All-Elder Chronicle

Storytellers who enjoy challenges may want to create and run a chronicle wherein all the characters are elders. The familiar elements of scale, scope, characters, plot and theme all take on significantly different dimensions when their focus is entirely on elders, and require some greater consideration. Depending on the type of story you're preparing, and the nature of your group, planning some escape routes in case things go wrong may well be the most important step in preparing to tell this kind of story.

The Elements of a Successful Elder Chronicle

Scale

The all-elder chronicle generally functions more smoothly with relatively few players. It is not unknown for games to consist of more than 50 players, or even several hundred when staged at conventions and the like. If you find that you'll have more than a dozen or so elder players, you may wish to reconsider — the more elders you include, the greater the potential for the game to get out of control on a regular basis. Fifty elders gathered in one place is an invitation to disaster, particularly when those elders have no one to lord it over but each other.

Limit your elder chronicle to a size that you feel you can comfortably handle. Attempting to narrate the titanic battle in a metropolis populated by a hundred Kindred with allegiances to different sects is a story best done with a large team of Storytellers and Narrators. If you decide to run a large elder chronicle, be certain you have enough Narrators and assistants to keep everything moving along. Elder interaction is complex at best, but the wheeling and dealing becomes almost Byzantine with a group of a dozen or more. So much political machination produces a significant amount of extra paperwork and record-keeping as you track all the shifts in ownership of Boons, Status Traits, Influences and alliances throughout the course of the game. Should disagreements between many elders lead to open violence, you and your Narrators will be very busy resolving all the challenges such conflict entails. You'll be grateful for the dozen or so Narrators following the latest challenges when you're in the middle of yet another Brujah-Ventrue rumble that's reducing the room to rubble.

Scope

Scope defines your chronicle's impact on the lives of your characters and the world in which they exist. You may choose to give your story a vast, sweeping scope, perhaps dealing with the fate of the world itself. Vampires who control governors, senators, ambassadors or even heads of state may influence the course of world events, bringing nations into armed conflict or completely restructuring the world economy to benefit their grand design. You might decide to focus your scope more narrowly, dealing with matters which interest only the individual characters. Such a chronicle might be the story of a small coterie of elders and their search for one of their number who's suddenly disappeared.

The chronicle's scope should be neither too trivial to merit the elders' attention, nor so overwhelming that they feel helpless and decide not even to bother trying. You may wish to vary the apparent scope throughout the progress of the story — the scope of events can be increased or decreased. For example, let's start with a story that involves an outside threat annexing the characters' mortal Influences. The elders eventually discover and confront the nemesis raiding their resources. After the threat is dealt with, the scope of the game can be refocused on the individual elders and their efforts to rebuild their damaged power bases. Some elders will almost certainly attempt to steal the Influences of their fellows rather than start over from scratch. The other elders may either fight the thief or decide to follow his example, igniting a citywide conflict which pits elder against elder, expanding the chronicle's scope once again. When elders from a neighboring city view this escalating warfare and decide it's the perfect time to annex the characters' city into their own domain, the scope increases again.

Be careful that the scope of your story doesn't expand until it reaches a point where it utterly dwarfs the characters, and players may prefer to throw up their hands in frustration rather than continue. Monitor the players' reactions to the chronicle, and use this information to help guide you in adjusting the scope to its best dramatic advantage. It's no fun when things are so huge that you feel you can't possibly make a difference.

When determining scope for this type of game, it is often useful to think of the elder chronicle as a single, brief segment in the ongoing story of these ancient creatures — a glimpse into one of the many possible tales which could be told of their long unlives. This doesn't

mean that you cannot run a chronicle wherein the stakes are nothing less than the fate of the world — just don't do it on a regular basis ("We're saving the world again? But we did that last week…."), and always do so with caution and with an eye toward balancing grandiose design with fundamental issues of character development.

Characters

It can be simpler to create premade characters complete with backgrounds, goals and motivations, and then to give these to your players before beginning your game. It is one way to make certain the characters' motivations are interlocked in order to guarantee the conflicts, alliances and intrigues which are the meat and drink of such stories. Read through the suggested elder motivations in Chapter One again, and think about which might be best suited to which characters. You will be able to come up with dozens of variations on these themes, and the more effort you put into this aspect, the more enjoyment you and your players will get from the story.

Are there Brujah and Ventrue elders in your chronicle? The natural rivalry of these clans can be greatly expanded when the characters are elders. Perhaps their current bitter enmity has its roots in a perpetually stalemated conflict that stretches across the centuries to medieval England, or perhaps it came about after Carthage's destruction. The two characters begin the chronicle with some common history and predetermined attitudes toward one another, which can jump-start a story. Is your story about the machinations of Sabbat leaders? Perhaps a Gangrel *antitribu* harbors a deep-seated grudge against the Lasombra bishop who has has blocked every opportunity for her advancement. Her fight with the bishop may be centuries old, but she can't confront her enemy openly without fear of reprisal. She dreams of retribution, and would give a lot to rub her tormentor's face in the dirt if the opportunity ever presented itself. The Lasombra bishop begins the game blissfully unaware of this long-bottled resentment and bitterness, but for how long?

Once you have assigned characters, it is up to the players to determine how they manifest their characters' motivations, goals and backgrounds. The background information you provide should be sufficiently clear and developed to assist them. Merely informing the Nosferatu elder that he despises all Ravnos is insufficient — detail the source of this hatred, and give the player something to work with as he considers how to interact with the Ravnos elder across the room.

Storytelling for Elders

The advantage of using ready-made characters is that it affords you a somewhat greater degree of control over the story. If you have a specific type of story in mind, pregenerated characters are the best method of steering events in the direction you wish. If your story hinges on awakening a torpid Methuselah under the city streets, you can increase the chances of players taking such action by providing one or more of them with characters whose goals include rousing this Methuselah from her eon-long sleep.

The drawback of utilizing ready-made characters is that players prefer to retain more creative freedom, particularly for a long chronicle. Some players object to the stereotypical attitudes and Traits of their characters' clans with premade characters, even if such motivations are critical to your planned course. Players can quickly become frustrated if forced to play characters they do not enjoy, and frustrated players can become destructive. For these reasons, confine premade characters to shorter chronicles.

Allowing players to create their own characters does not mean that they should do so in a vacuum, nor that they have *carte blanche* during the creation process. Set your boundaries and stick to them. If you have decided that Followers of Set are inappropriate to the story you are telling (because they are the primary antagonists or some such), inform the group of this restriction before they start creating characters. Tell them what sort of story you're planning for and what they need to think about, such as that your city is Camarilla-controlled, that independents need a very good reason for appearing in the city, etc.

Each character should have a strong motive that is clear to both the player and you; it will be invaluable when creating subplots. If your players need help, suggest that they consider their elders in a vacuum — what would their characters wish to accomplish if they were the sole Kindred in the story, unopposed by rivals and free to do exactly as they pleased? Would they want to be left completely alone in quiet contemplation as they pursue Golconda, or would they want to secure control over every factory and manufacturing plant in the city? Now ask the players to think about these motivations in relation to the same setting, but accounting for the presence of other Kindred in the city. Does the reality of sharing the night with other elders change these goals, or does it mean that the characters must discover new means of accomplishing their goals? This kind of exercise not only helps the players build strong character motivations, but helps set the stage for dynamic interactions when play begins.

It's best to begin an all-elder chronicle with characters at the lowest power level possible. If you allow the players characters who are each capable of leveling entire city blocks single-handedly, you have no one to blame but yourself if your chronicle concludes with the characters' untimely deaths or the extinction of all life on the planet. Unless the plot of your chronicle involves Gehenna, you probably are not planning for this kind of outcome for your story.

Encourage players to give their elders distinct personalities, interesting histories and several weaknesses. After all, for all the age and power these beings possess, they are hardly perfect. Give players enough information about the scope, setting and basic structure of the chronicle so that they can make appropriate choices in these matters. One who decides that her Nosferatu elder witnessed firsthand the formation of the Soviet Union, starting with the Russian Revolution, will be irked if she unexpectedly discovers during the first session that you have rewritten history and removed that particular event in the process.

Perhaps the most important contribution you can make during character creation is to encourage players to think the way an elder thinks. The life span of an elder vampire is prolonged many, many times beyond a human's, and yet our human perceptions, ideas and impressions are the tools we use when designing a character whose fundamental concept is very different from our own. The physical, mental and social capabilities that make elders distinct from neonates and ancillae manifest themselves through roleplay. Encourage the players to imagine how their characters watched or participated in the pageant of history, how that pageant has affected their outlook, and how they'll reflect that in play.

Plot

The scale, scope, theme and mood of an elder chronicle are all important to its success, but the plot is the heart and soul which allows your chronicle to move. The Storyteller is responsible for creating an engaging, progressive series of events which involve all the players, and strives to capture their imaginations. Composing a successful plot for an all-elder chronicle is no simple task. If you make the plot too obvious or simple, the players will solve things too quickly and become bored; if you create a story too difficult and nebulous, they may become frustrated at their slow progress. Balance is the key to a successful plot — your story must be sufficiently complex and interesting to offer the players a

Storytelling for Elders

challenge, but should also be tailored to their individual characters in such a way that they each have opportunities to advance the plot.

You should have the basic elements of your plot in mind so you can assist players during character creation. If you have established a chronicle which revolves around an elite Sabbat strike force cut off from help deep within the heart of Camarilla territory, it is doubtful that Camarilla-loyal Ventrue and Toreador elders would fare well in this story.

Construct your plot on several levels, both macro and micro. The macro-level, or main plot, should revolve around events, ideas or situations which involve the entire group. This is the foundation of your story, and should be appropriately related to the theme, mood and scale you chose (see above). All the elders should have the opportunity to participate to some degree in this main plot, although the characters' own actions largely determine the level of involvement they have. It is perfectly acceptable to let the macro-level of plot be rather obvious — this doesn't mean it should be trite or clichéd, but rather that it is fine to make the main element of the story obvious to the characters, since this is what will initially attract their attention.

The micro-level of your story consists of subplots, most of which should be designed with individual characters in mind. These are the tales and events which are created for, and are sustained by, particular characters in your chronicle. A Nosferatu elder may wish to extend the boundaries of his sewer domain, or a Toreador elder may desire to humble a long-time rival. You should have no difficulty in constructing subplots for your elders, but be certain to involve your elders in some of the subplot planning. This will ensure that each participant is comfortable in the subplot you and she create. You may wish to establish a romantic subplot for the elder Malkavian *antitribu*, but unless the person playing the Malkavian *antitribu* is comfortable with the idea, the result may be an inadequate subplot and an annoyed player.

Use particular care when playing a chronicle with pregenerated elders. You must supply all the subplots for such characters, and you must make certain that the micro-level of the story meshes properly. Suppose you create a Tzimisce elder who has been pursuing his packmate's assassin for over a century, and is by the start of the chronicle nearly consumed with the terrible thirst for vengeance. Imagine how disappointed the Tzimisce elder's player will be if he plays through the duration of an extended chronicle without gaining even the opportunity to confront the assassin, simply because you did not include the killer among the player characters or Narrator characters. His entire

motivation as a character remains unfulfilled for the duration of the chronicle, and he may well feel dissatisfied by the result.

Plot creation for the all-elder chronicle need not be the sole responsibility of the Storyteller. Players should be invited to share in the establishment of the micro-level of the story as well. The Storyteller must create the main plot as the framework for the tale, but the players should feel encouraged to add support and strength to the framework through the creation of some of their own subplots. Once again, this stage of preparation should be a joint venture between Storyteller and players. A player may choose to play a Ventrue elder in your chronicle, and will be eager to play out her own subplot concerning her character's flight from her former comrades, a notorious Sabbat pack. This is without a doubt a juicy and interesting subplot, but the Storyteller must know about it in order to make effective use of the information!

When making final preparations for your elder chronicle, consider how you will set in motion and maintain a plot with a controlled level of conflict. The story setting should change sufficiently over the course of the chronicle to remain interesting, and for the conflicts themselves to matter (see Scope, above), but should also be stable enough to be sustainable throughout many game sessions. Otherwise, you may find that the elders' interaction with the plot creates problems your group will then look to you to solve (see Troubleshooting for Elders, below).

Theme

Storytellers whose chronicles feature an all-elder group may choose any theme for their story, but care should be taken to select themes with special relevance to elder characters. Revenge, for example, is an excellent theme to explore in an elder chronicle. What happens to beings who thirst for, or are the target of, more than their fair share of vengeance throughout their lives? Do they ever weary of seeking vengeance for insults, or do they develop some type of protective mental attitude against such trifles? Who really benefits from revenge? What happens to an elder who spends her unlife seeking revenge and finally obtains it? What forms might the revenge of an angered elder take? The Storyteller might also choose the theme of loyalty for her story. At what price can elders expect or demand loyalty? Can loyalty between elders ever truly last? Do expectations of loyalty inevitably result in betrayal? Why does loyalty seem to be among the most fleeting of the Kindred's characteristics? What happens when we refuse to offer loyalty when it is expected or demanded?

Sample Elder Chronicle

The characters comprise the primogen of a moderately sized city under the control of a newly installed prince. The former prince and primogen were ousted by a conclave after archons discovered alarming cracks in the city's Masquerade. The new primogen must strive to deal with the problems left by their predecessors in addition to their personal issues and the night-to-night challenges of running a city. The elders' motivations will be of paramount importance in determining how the characters interact with one another, in addition to exploring how they proceed to rebuild the shattered Masquerade and bring the city under control.

Sometimes a seemingly simple plot can be a springboard for any number of interesting subplots, particularly in an all-elder chronicle. This sample plot is a strong but flexible framework to which you can attach an almost endless variety of story adornments to flesh out the idea. This basic story can be expanded in any number of directions. For example:

• What happened to the previous prince and primogen? If the conclave spared their lives, they could be intent on reclaiming their lost authority. This sets up a politically motivated chronicle, charged with tension as the two factions attempt to prove the other's incompetence and malfeasance. If the former rulers of the city are desperate, they may even go as far as to exacerbate the problems they created in an attempt to demonstrate that their successors are no better equipped to run the city than they themselves were.

• Perhaps it is too late, and the thin veil of the Masquerade has been irrevocably pierced by the keen eyes of vampire-hunters. Agents of the Inquisition or the federal government could be establishing their presence in the city by the time your characters assume control of their new domain. The characters will become the hunters' quarry in the nights to come, and must find a means of thwarting the hunters or suffer a fate even worse than that of their predecessors.

• Factions who have waited patiently for a sign of weakness may choose this opportunity to strike. An anarch gang or Sabbat pack may select the changing of the guard as the perfect moment to attack, hoping to cause sufficient confusion that the new rulers will not be able to mount a defense or counterattack. Introducing a group of antagonists need not mean locating more players; the activities of the gang or pack can easily take place "offstage" as the antagonists assault the elders' holdings and resources.

Twists, surprises and layers of intrigue add depth and interest to what was a relatively uncomplicated plot structure.

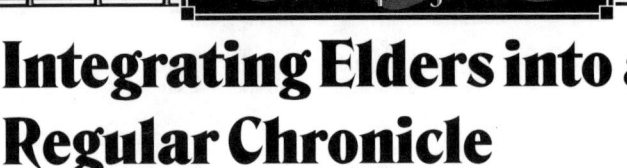

Laws of Elysium

Integrating Elders into a Regular Chronicle

Many Storytellers who read this book will already be engaged in running a chronicle, but will wish to incorporate some of the ideas and concepts they read here into the story. Does this mean that you must scrap the current chronicle and start an entirely new story, or that you must rewrite your entire plot and subplots in order to accommodate elder characters? Not at all. With some conscientious effort, you can smoothly integrate elders into an established chronicle. Add new elders into your regular chronicle sparingly. Dropping one or two elders into a game in progress can increase dramatic tension and give the plot a richer texture. Introducing too many new elders can create chaos.

Before adding an elder to your chronicle, examine the current plot and consider the effect a new elder will have on it. How will the incoming elder alter the existing story elements (for they are almost certain to change once she is introduced). How will you go about casting the new role? Will you give the player a pregenerated elder to ensure that the new character meshes with your chronicle, or will you allow her to create her own character within the guidelines you supply? If you've already spent a great deal of time in crafting the chronicle, you should be able to identify the types of problems you are likely to encounter, and what kind of preventive medicine is in order.

The existing plot of your regular chronicle is probably already a challenge for your current players. Is it also of sufficient interest to the arriving elder? Will the presence of a new elder completely invalidate the plot, or will the story be enhanced? The plot might well be of less interest to the elder than her own personal goals, in which case you should identify which of the existing storylines her goals might intersect with. Will this contribute to the game?

An example of a chronicle which easily could be derailed by the introduction of an elder concerns a coterie of neonate anarchs who are trying to overthrow the prince. The neonates are singly far less powerful than the elder, and even collectively might have difficulty in preserving their safety. How will these anarchs react to the sudden appearance of a Tremere elder who offers to assist them? Attempting to integrate this particular elder into that particular chronicle might not be such a wise idea. Why should the neonates believe that a

Storytelling for Elders

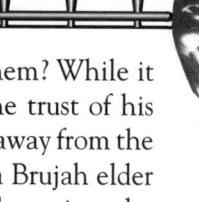

Tremere, much less an elder, would be interested in them? While it might be interesting to see how the Tremere gains the trust of his young compatriots, it could also drag out and take time away from the main plotline. A better choice might be to introduce a Brujah elder who wants to guide the young anarchs in their struggle against the oppressive status quo, or to urge them to use nonviolent means to get what they want from the prince.

Perhaps you have set up a framework regarding the efforts of a Camarilla-held city to root out invading Setites who have established a temple in the vicinity. Currently, the characters are making steady progress in discovering the existence of the Setites and the location of their lair. Now that the enemy has been found, the characters must decide how to deal with the threat. Does the about-to-be-introduced elder possess any Abilities or Disciplines which, if utilized, will suddenly make this task too simple? If so, it isn't necessary to scrap the main plot completely, but consider revising some of the remaining portions of the story to ensure that it continues at the proper pace and remains interesting for the players. You might decide, for instance, to change the manner in which the Setites are infiltrating the city, making them more difficult to discover, or you might improve the defenses around their temple if the elder is persuaded to join the assault.

You must also give some attention to the effect of the elders on the individual subplots which are currently in progress throughout your game. Will the elder change the scope or viability of any of these personal storylines? Can the elder be safely and effectively introduced into any of these subplots? Consider two characters deeply enamored of one another. If the elder is added into this relationship, it creates a love triangle with a multitude of new possibilities. The elder may possess motivations and goals similar to those of one or more existing characters, establishing a potential for conflict that you must determine how best to manage. Two Toreador ancillae may combine their resources to obtain control over an important civic institution, such as a city orchestra. Introducing an elder Ventrue who possesses the desire and resources to snatch the orchestra right out of the Toreadors' grasp guarantees a new twist to your story. What happens if the Toreador decide to unite the rest of the clan against the Ventrue usurper, or if they hire a mercenary Assamite to do him in?

You may decide to introduce the elder as a new antagonist — a Nosferatu *antitribu*, for example, who has recently arrived in the city for the dual purpose of exchanging information with his Camarilla

Laws of Elysium

counterparts and rescuing a fellow Sabbat vampire from the prince's sheriff. The Nosferatu is unlikely to march into the Prince's court and announce his plans to all and sundry, even if this approach saves a great deal of exposition time. The same holds true if the elder is intent on a peaceful mission, such as the pursuit of a fragment of ancient lore which might lead him a step closer to his goal of achieving Golconda. An elder Kindred would not survive long if she made a habit of revealing her true agenda to everyone she met. An elder's business is her own, and she is within her rights to inform the nosy little neonates to buzz off. Of course, that will probably only serve to pique the players' interest — what reason could an elder have for being in the city?

Neonate and ancillae characters tend to gravitate toward elders, and you must take this fact into account when integrating an elder into your chronicle. If an elder and ancilla are of the same clan, it is understandable that the latter may feel some measure of kinship with the elder and wish to introduce himself to the newcomer. The Ventrue elder who enters a domain controlled primarily by Clan Brujah will certainly find herself the focus of a great deal of neonate attention from the very first night. Younger characters sometimes hope to request favors of their elders, and sometimes they plan to ride their coattails. Sometimes they seek another voice to involve in the simmering cauldron of local politics, and other times they hope to gain a new ally (or perhaps a convenient scapegoat for an impending fracture of the Masquerade). Neonates may be awestruck by these living relics, and approach them for advice or guidance (such as how to live as long as they have). Ancillae may find them a welcome voice of experience after dealing with neonates for so long (even though they themselves are now the "neonate" in the eyes of the elder). If the elder's Nature and Demeanor permit it, encourage the player occasionally to dispense a few in-character snippets of advice or praise to the "deserving youngsters." Such interaction can make the difference between a smooth transition and an unwelcome intrusion.

Elders will most likely experience difficulty in steering clear of any prominent plot threads you have already woven into your chronicle. Indeed, it would be a very strange thing not to be approached by any younger vampires regarding some mystery or problem. Should an elder truly wish to remain aloof from a given plot or subplot, she may well be obliged to extricate herself continuously from difficult or even compromising positions. Requesting that one's fellow Kindred leave

Storytelling for Elders

one alone often has the exact reverse effect, making the elder the direct center of plenty of unwanted attention — the assumption being, of course, that anyone who asks to be left alone has something to hide, and anyone who has something to hide is worth observing. Elder characters (and players) should accept the fact that they will be subject to a certain degree of scrutiny and attention from their fellow Kindred, and should determine how they would react to these circumstances before they enter the chronicle.

Elder Plot Hooks

- **Rivals** — There is nothing like good old-fashioned rivalry to stir up plenty of character-related conflict. If you plan to introduce more than one new elder into your regular chronicle simultaneously, consider providing them with a sufficient reason to view one another as competitors. Each elder should have some element in her background which intersects with the others, and those playing these elders should make an attempt to work out the idiosyncrasies of their relationship prior to joining the game in progress.

- **Clan Matters** — An effective means of introducing an elder into an ongoing chronicle is to make the character a representative of her clan bearing a message or instructions for the other members of her clan already in the city. Her own orders are to remain in the city and assist her clan in achieving its goals in this area.

- **Traitor** — The elder is a traitor and is fleeing those she betrayed. Perhaps she is a renegade Tremere seeking refuge from the minions of the Council of Seven, or maybe she is a Brujah anarch who failed to come to the aid of her pack and now attempts to escape their wrath. Consider if her treason is meant to engender sympathy or rage, and tailor the motive to be appropriately believable.

- **Archons** — The elder characters are a coterie of archons, the brood of a Justicar charged with enforcing the Masquerade and hunting diablerists. Rather than announce their identity and station to the prince, they arrive secretly in the city and pose as ordinary Kindred. Once established, they quietly begin investigating the other characters for potential breaches of the Traditions.

- **Infiltrator** — Much like the archon suggestion described above, the elder is a Sabbat pack leader intent on recruiting new members from among the city's anarchs and disgruntled Kindred.

- **Prince's Lackey** — If the elder character is of the appropriate clan and sect affiliation, she can be introduced as a new functionary of,

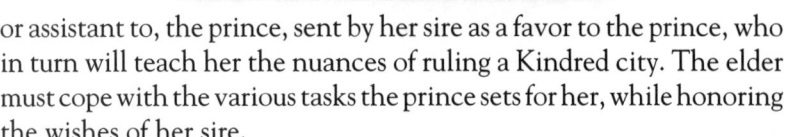

Laws of Elysium

or assistant to, the prince, sent by her sire as a favor to the prince, who in turn will teach her the nuances of ruling a Kindred city. The elder must cope with the various tasks the prince sets for her, while honoring the wishes of her sire.

• **Methuselah Agent** — The elder character is the spy of an ancient vampire who has only recently awakened from torpor. The Methuselah needs to know many details about how the world has changed since she slept, and what the Kindred of the city are now doing around her. The elder will probably be obliged to ask many questions and become interested in almost every aspect of the chronicle in order to fulfill the Methuselah's commands.

• **Prince** — This particular plot hook works best in a city without a current prince or with a prince whose popularity is on the wane. An elder who arrives in the city to announce her claim to domain, or to usurp the throne of the current prince, can galvanize the Kindred of a city into action either on her behalf or against her.

Troubleshooting for Elders

Your most potent defense against losing control of the chronicle is restraint. By now you will have seen that many players often enjoy creating the most powerful characters they can. This tendency to gravitate toward powerful characters is a condition endemic to roleplaying in general, and to **The Masquerade** in particular. Be prepared for requests and the occasional begging for characters and powers you know will upset your chronicle, but which the player wants in spite of your most persuasive arguments. Players want the "best" character — it's a given in human nature — but too many players equate "best" with "most powerful" rather than "most interesting" or "most challenging." If you ask someone why he wants to play a sixth-generation Brujah with the maximum number of Attribute, Willpower and Ability Traits, and he answers, "Because it's fun," chances are he means, "Because I'm tired of getting womped on, and I want to start womping now." This type of player is not telling a story or roleplaying — he's in a competition between himself and the other players. He believes that this game has winners and losers, that the winner is the player whose character is the last one standing at the end of the night, and he wants to be a winner. No matter what it takes, he wants to be a winner. Killing characters, derailing plot, driving you insane — whatever it takes to be a winner.

Storytelling for Elders

Restrain the impulse to give in to such requests; you'll regret it when your story runs awry and new players are driven off by "Godzilla." It can be tempting to give in to player requests (or demands), particularly if the player threatens to quit the game or disrupt the current chronicle. If you know that the player's request is unacceptable because it will unbalance your chronicle, stick to your guns as the Storyteller looking out for your game. The enjoyment of your player *group* is more important than appeasing someone who is apparently not mature enough to participate in your story.

Another line of defense is clarity. It is up to you to remind the players of their responsibilities when playing elders, whether your story is comprised solely of elders or a mixture of power levels. Even as you strive to live up to your own responsibilities as the Storyteller, so must the elders cooperate with you in fulfilling their end of the bargain. Tell your elders exactly what you expect from them and what you see as their responsibilities to the story. Perhaps you don't want the elders to interfere with a particular subplot you've crafted for a new player who is trying out the game for the first time — too much attention from, or the untimely intervention of, the elders might overwhelm him, ending his interest in the game and depriving your troupe of a new member. Maybe you have decided that all elders must begin the game with an extra Beast Trait, or must possess no more than the usual Abilities or Influence Traits. Regardless of the exact stipulations, communicate these conditions to your elder players and make certain they acknowledge your expectations. Be as clear as possible when expressing your concerns, and allow the elders ample opportunity to ask questions. Armed with a mutual understanding of the elders' places and roles in the chronicle, you can reasonably minimize the initial problems you might otherwise face.

What happens if you unintentionally miscalculate the appropriate power level for your all-elder chronicle, or allow a player to play an elder too powerful for the existing plot? The danger signs are easy to identify:

• Elders seem intent on turning every minor disagreement with other characters into lethal showdowns.

• Game sessions frequently degenerate into prolonged mob combats during which the noncombatants are particularly bored and unhappy.

Laws of Elysium

- Players appear intoxicated with the power of their characters and act irresponsibly, disregarding the Masquerade and relying on their elder powers to save them even from blatantly foolhardy actions.
- Key story elements are ignored or discarded in favor of Physical Challenges and combat.
- Players ask you to "do something" about a particular player whom they feel is causing disruption by the manner in which he portrays his elder.
- Characters die with an alarming frequency at the hands of elders.

You might be tempted to raise the power level even higher in order to correct one or more of these undesirable situations — in a word, don't. It is false logic to conclude that the threat of mutually assured destruction between characters will act as a deterrent. You might think that introducing even more powerful characters will slow down this kind of behavior or prevent it altogether, but you will find that power escalation only increases the frequency of disruption. Examine the problem and analyze what you perceive to be its cause before deciding exactly how best to handle it.

Sometimes, hosting a "post-mortem" discussion with your troupe after the conclusion of a night's game can give you some insight into the cause of any problems you perceived. Talk freely about the characters' actions and their motivations — your players may surprise you with their explanations for their characters' behavior. If their motives don't wash, decide what you want to do about the situation. You could decide that your players simply aren't ready for the privilege and responsibility of playing characters of this power level. If this is the case, try starting over with less powerful characters. Talk with the players you feel are most disruptive and discuss their behavior. Maybe they play the game simply for the rumbles, and are not happy with your more intrigue-oriented plots. If you believe a single player is at the root of these difficulties, give him the option of modifying his behavior or leaving the game. Don't sacrifice your enjoyment, and that of everyone else, for the sake of one disruptive player. If after a reasonable attempt at correction the same problems recur, you may be playing with the wrong troupe.

Remember to keep an open mind and be flexible. Accept that your players will stray from the story, miss clues and take the game in unforeseen directions — that's part of telling a story. Because of the difference in power between elders, ancillae and neonates, the elders

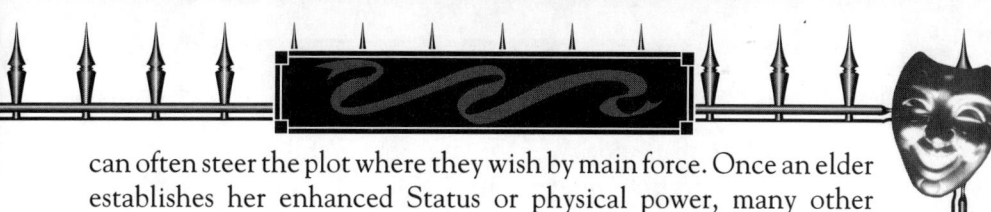

can often steer the plot where they wish by main force. Once an elder establishes her enhanced Status or physical power, many other characters are less inclined to refuse to carry out her wishes, reasoning that it's better to relinquish the clue to the elder rather to have one's face pulped or memory erased. In other instances, elder characters can unintentionally create circumstances which alter the entire dynamic of your chronicle. A Malkavian neonate with a crucial clue falls afoul of the Nosferatu elder. He takes her down to the sewers for a prolonged "visit" to teach her better manners; meanwhile, the clock is running down, her coterie is frantic, and the clue which could have unlocked the plot is missing in action.

If this sort of thing seems to happen frequently, try to find out if the players in question are simply acting out what they believe to be an interpretation of their characters' motivations and Nature, or if they are pursuing some nongame-related goals which are dampening the fun for everyone else. Did the prince decide unexpectedly to execute a character for a ridiculously minor offense? Talk with him after the game, and be honest about your concerns. It's possible he felt he was portraying a Derangement accurately and skillfully; maybe he was so caught up in the ebb and flow of the plot that he forgot to be respectful of other players. If you maintain strong, constant lines of communication with your players, you should be able to approach them and discuss such topics without making them feel defensive. Publicly berating players for seemingly inappropriate actions doesn't do anything other than antagonize the players and make you look foolish. If you discover that the elder players believe themselves to be acting in accordance with your stated expectations and within the boundaries of their established motivations and goals, fixing any problems should simply be a matter of altering some of the plot elements as discussed above.

Should you find that the elder characters are indeed acting outside the initial dictates of their character concepts and motivations — creating new personal subplots, for example, without meaning to disrupt the game — your task is somewhat more of a problem. It's best to involve some or all of the elder characters in finding a solution to this type of situation. Asking a particular elder to avoid interfering with a certain subplot might be somewhat inelegant, but might also maintain your chronicle's viability. If you are certain that an elder character's unintentional effect on the story is disruptive or harmful, you should feel secure in asking that

player to help you guide the plot in a more useful direction. Some Storytellers refrain from ever interfering in the chronicle's direction once it is set in motion, preferring to adopt a more *laissez faire* relationship to the plot once it is underway and to let the tale grow in the telling. This strategy sometimes works for chronicles wherein the characters collectively do not have the power to disrupt significantly the flow of the plot. Even when your players roleplay responsibly, their actions can still send the plot off course. You must keep track of where the plot is going, otherwise you may find the chronicle ends abruptly and in a manner far less satisfying than you originally intended. It's not about whether or not to let the bus run driverless, but rather about applying sufficient guidance and direction to ensure that everyone on the bus reaches the destination with the maximum amount of fun and enjoyment.

If you determine that a player is using the power of his elder character to ride roughshod over your plot and lord it over the other players because he enjoys doing so, you must deal with him immediately before things go too far. Talk privately and candidly with the problem player. If you believe he has the potential to learn to roleplay responsibly and to respect the other players, by all means try to allow him to continue to play an elder character, perhaps with the assistance of a trusted Narrator, or you may consider challenging him with a significantly less powerful, but no less interesting, character. If he chooses not to mend his ways, ask him not to return to the game. This can be uncomfortable, but in these circumstances it is to the long-term benefit of yourself and your players.

Character Advancement

Players who do not currently play elders will want to play them eventually, particularly if you introduce them into your regular chronicle. Meanwhile, your elders players will want to advance their own characters. You'll be inundated with requests to grant more experience points, to permit neonate characters to rise to elder status, and to allow the chronicle to progress in time to the point where previously young characters are now wearing the mantle of elder. There are several techniques you can use to guide character advancement, and all require some measure of restraint on your part, tempered with the acceptance that characters are not static but ever-changing entities, just like the people who play them.

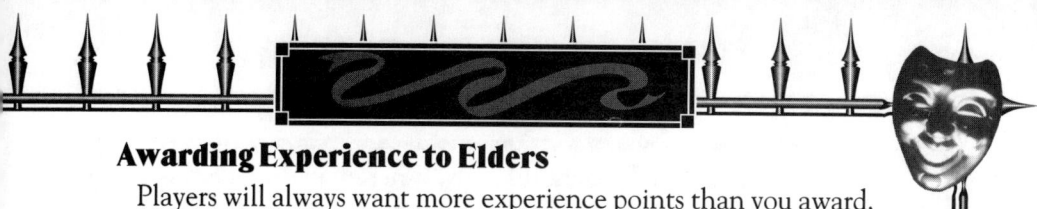

Awarding Experience to Elders

Players will always want more experience points than you award, and you will always want to make certain that characters do not advance too quickly. Players may argue that elders are older and therefore smarter, and should therefore learn now powers and skills more quickly than non-elders, so why not give them a few more experience points per game session? In truth, these aged Kindred find that learning new concepts and skills becomes far more difficult with the passing of the centuries. The elders are the guardians of the status quo — change in Kindred society is anathema to them, and this staunch opposition to change manifests itself in their ability to learn new things and cope with new ideas. Advancements which move like quicksilver through the younger, more receptive Kindred mind and body flow sluggishly through the barriers of mental and physical resistance. Thus, the older the Kindred, the more difficult it is for her to increase her powers and capabilities.

Increasing the necessary experience point expenditures for elders based on the characters' age reflects the increased difficulty the elder vampire experiences in attempting to advance his abilities. Recognize that elders who advance faster than, or even at the equivalent rate of, non-elders will pose serious problems sooner rather than later. Elders usually begin with more Traits and Disciplines than non-elder characters. If you permit elders to advance faster than non-elders, or even at the same rate, the power differential will only become that much greater. Conversely, don't advance the non-elder characters so quickly that the 13th-generation neonate Gangrel who was Embraced five years ago can singlehandedly thrash the eighth-generation elder Tremere, embraced many centuries ago, in only a month's worth of games. Such progress should be moderate to slow, and amended by your better judgment if you believe things are advancing too fast or too slow.

Awarding elders too many experience points can lead to the elders becoming overconfident in their own abilities or omnipotent, damaging the game for everyone involved. Allowing elders to stock up on Advanced and Master-level powers too quickly creates a game wherein they are almost impossible to deal with — they begin to cause huge waves with the smallest gestures, casually destroying characters and subplots with equal ease. Restraint and balance are the keys to preventing this disaster, and you should exercise them ceaselessly. If you must err when advancing a character, it is best to err on the side of caution.

Laws of Elysium

This chart reflects the difficulty inherent in the elder's skill advancement. Locate the elder's chronological age on the first column. The subsequent columns establish the experience point costs for new Attribute Traits, Ability Traits, Disciplines and the removal of Negative Traits.

Character's age	New Attribute	New Ability	New Clan Discipline
201-350	3	2	B 4, I 7, A 10
351-500	4	3	B 4, I 7, A 10
501-650	5	4	B 5, I 8, A 11
651-800	6	5	B 5, I 8, A 11
801-950	7	6	B 6, I 9, A 12
951-1000	8	7	B 6, I 9, A 12
1001+	9	8	B 7, I 10, A 13
901+	10	9	B 8, I, 11, A 14

B = Basic, I = Intermediate, A = Advanced

Character's age	Raise Ability	Non-Clan Discipline	Remove Negative Trait
201-350	2	B 5, I 8, A 11	3
351-500	2	B 5, I 8, A 11	4
501-650	3	B 6, I 9, A 12	5
651-800	3	B 6, I 9, A 12	6
801-950	4	B 7, I 10, A 13	7
951-1000	4	B 7, I 10, A 13	8
1001+	5	B 8, I 11, A 14	9

Pretenders

Pretenders are vampires who are elder in generation but not necessarily in age. Such Kindred are only technically considered "elders" in the eyes of their more experienced peers, especially those who have existed far longer than any Pretender. However, Kindred emphasize respect for purity of bloodline, and thus Pretenders are grudgingly admitted into elder society due to the power of the vitae flowing through their veins. Pretenders are honored for their lineage, not for themselves. Examples of Pretenders are those Kindred who were recently Embraced by powerful sires, granting them the privilege of unusually low generation, or those sinister vampires who have committed the heinous crime of diablerie and stolen the power of their elders.

Storytelling for Elders

Players who wish to create Pretender characters should follow the character creation system outlined in **Laws of the Night**, with the following modifications:

• Pretenders start at 10th Generation, and may lower their generation further by means of Negative Traits. No Pretender may start with a generation lower than eighth.

• Pretenders receive the additional Status Trait *Known*.

• All Pretenders are automatically one Trait down in any Social Challenge involving a true elder.

Pretenders should be prepared to receive some degree of animosity and reluctance from their true elder peers. Camarilla Kindred may confine their distaste for Pretenders to social sniping and snide remarks about the character's age, but the scorn of Sabbat vampires may take on far more ugly connotations.

Time-lapse Advancement

Some chronicles are designed to span decades or even longer periods of time. They may begin, for example, during the Enlightenment and continue through the present day, with each game session representing a number of years, decades or centuries. During such chronicles it is inevitable that some characters will achieve elder status simply by virtue of their survival. Characters who become elders should naturally experience some degree of improvement over their abilities and skills, depending on what they have accomplished and on how much time has passed during the chronicle. You must decide exactly how to handle the progression to elder status for your players. There are two useful methods to facilitate this process.

Method One: Start the characters as neonates when the chronicle commences. At the conclusion of each game session that reflects a transition into the next era when the characters are active, award them each a certain number of experience points. The characters may spend their experience points on whatever enhancements they wish during the transition.

Method Two: Begin the characters on their journey as in Method One, above. Decide how much time will pass in your chronicle, and establish the appropriate transition periods. When you reach a transitional stage, award your players experience points as you normally would for this type of story. However, permit them to spend their experience primarily on those skills and capabilities they managed to use successfully during the last portion of the chronicle.

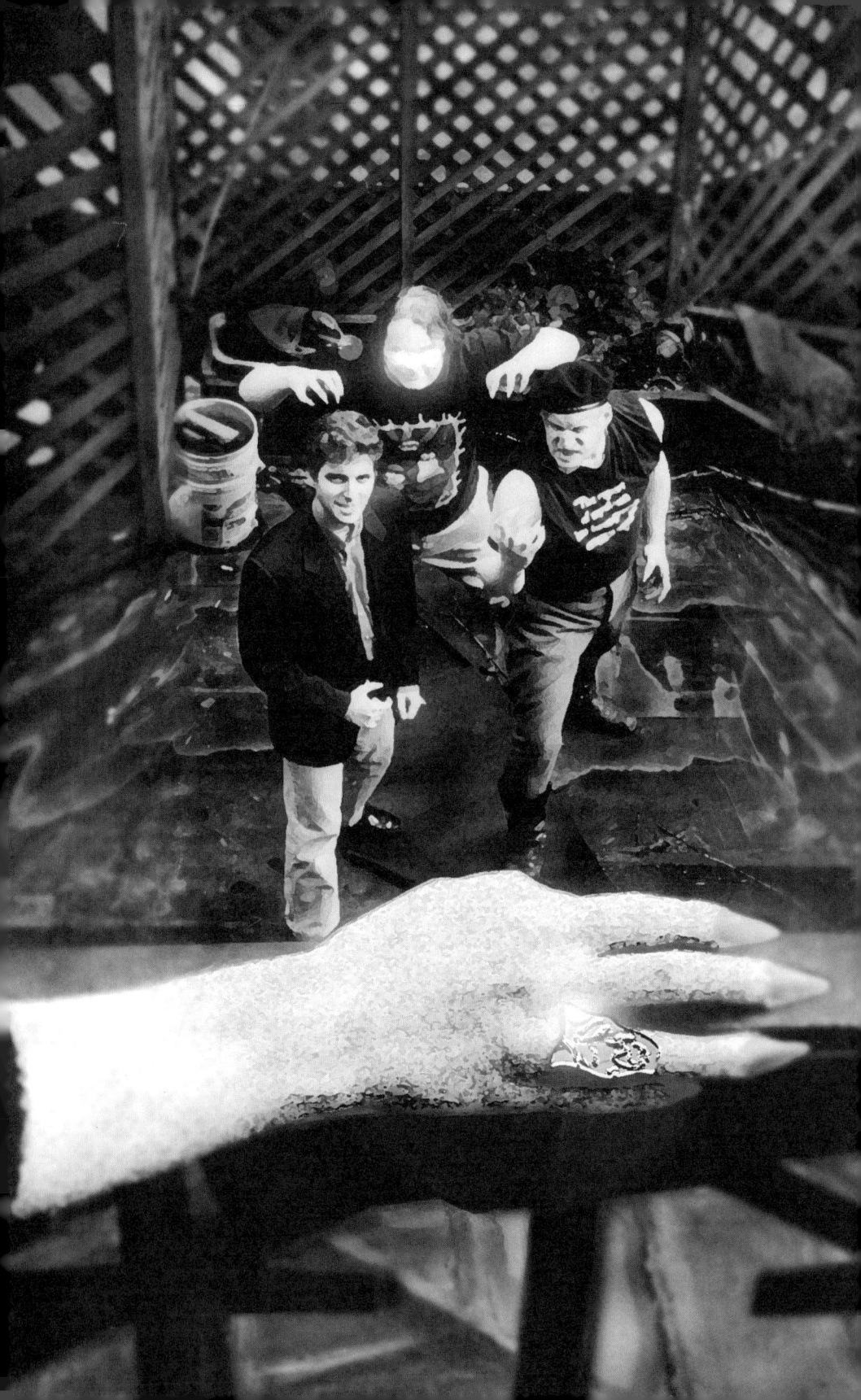

Appendix

New Rules and Clarifications

Blood

Blood Addiction

Lupine blood is addictive to Kindred. Whenever a Kindred feeds from a Lupine, he must conduct a Static Mental Challenge, with the difficulty being the sum of the Lupine's current Rage and Gnosis Traits. If the Kindred wins, he is free from addiction; if he loses, he gains the Derangement *Addicted*, and must feed from Lupine blood whenever possible. Failure to feed thus on a regular basis may provoke frenzy, sending the Kindred after the closest Lupine. Kindred that become addicted to Lupine blood may attempt to "kick the habit" by expending a Willpower Trait and retesting the initial Static Challenge. This retest may be attempted only *once*, and failure means that you automatically frenzy on the Derangement.

Blood Expenditures

Blood expenditure limitations are valid in all cases *except* where a Discipline would otherwise require a vampire to spend more blood than his generation would allow. In such cases, the Kindred can use blood in excess of generation limits, but *only* for purposes of activating that Discipline.

In other words, a vampire with *Form of the Beast* may spend the three Traits of blood in order to change instantly to the form desired, but may not spend blood for any other reason until the next turn — about a minute or so.

Blood Storage

To store mortal blood successfully (as opposed to coming home to a refrigerator full of clotted gunk), a character must have a minimum *Medical* Ability rating of two or at least one level of the *Health* Influence. Human blood, under proper conditions, can be stored for one month. Then, even under the best of circumstances, it goes bad. Drinking bad blood renders no nourishment, and may induce the vampire to vomit up good blood already in his system.

Kindred vitae has radically different properties than does mortal blood. Carefully stored, it can provide nourishment and pleasure (or bonding) for quite some time. Neonate blood rarely lasts more than one year, while a Methuselah's blood does not lose potency for a century, if not longer.

Note: Questions of blood potency also apply to drinks left for Kindred in torpor.

Blood Traits of Food Source

The following chart lists the number of Blood Traits found in various creatures. If a food source is drained completely it dies, with the exception of Garou, who lose one Health Level for every two Blood Traits taken. Humans and animals lose two Health Levels per Trait taken, and die if completely drained.

Food Source	Blood Traits
Cat	1
Chicken	1
Child	2
Cow	8
Dog	2
Garou	8
Human	4
Rat	1

Appendix

Willpower

Replenishing Willpower

Willpower is replenished in full once the Storyteller determines the story is over. The process of replenishment takes precisely as long as the Storyteller says it does.

Staying Awake

The expenditure of Willpower is required for a vampire to remain awake during the day. This has nothing to with being able to move about normally in the daylight — a vampire must spend Willpower to move, even in the darkest, dankest crypt, *as long as the sun is in the sky overhead.* If a vampire wishes to remain awake during daylight hours, he must spend one Willpower Trait for every four hours after sunrise during which he wants to stomp around. Obviously, given this restriction, a vampire can't stay up all day too often.

Frenzy

A Willpower Trait may be spent to prevent frenzy for 10 minutes. If the character has not removed herself from the situation, person or object provoking her at the end of that time, she must spend another Willpower Trait to stave off the inevitable for another 10 minutes. This continues until either the character is away from the provocation, she runs out of Willpower or she gives in and frenzies.

Replenishing Traits

Once per night, a character may choose to spend a Willpower Trait and regain all lost Traits in any of the three Attribute categories (Social, Physical, Mental). This does not mean that a character may spend a Willpower Trait and regain all lost Traits in all categories; a Willpower Trait must be spent for each category the character wishes replenished. The expenditure is limited to one per category per night.

Ignoring Wounds

Those characters without *Endurance* may find themselves in dire straits if they have sustained wounds. The expenditure of one Willpower Trait allows a character to ignore all wound penalties for one challenge. Characters with *Celerity* should note that each additional action is a separate challenge, and requires a new Willpower Trait to be spent for each action in which the character wishes to negate his wound penalties.

Laws of Elysium

The Long Night

The following Disciplines apply to the clans and bloodlines found in **The Long Night**.

Abombwe

Master

Devil-Channel

With the expenditure of two Blood Traits, you may channel your Beast to concentrate in a specific area of your body. The concentration of Beast-nature manifests itself as a film of black, clotted blood covering the appropriate body part. The Beast may only be forced into one spot at a time; one cannot *Devil-Channel* into one's hands and throat simultaneously.

Hands: You may now inflict aggravated damage with your bare, bloody hands. You also gain the Physical Trait *Tough* for the five minutes during which this power is active.

Torso: You may now use your Blood Traits more efficiently. While using this power, you double the number of Physical Traits you can gain through using blood.

Throat: Your voice is now terrifying, so much so that on a successful Social Challenge all mortals must flee you for 10 minutes. Awakened beings are down two Traits in any challenge involving you for the next 10 minutes if you beat them in a Social Challenge while using this power.

Feet: By stamping your feet on the ground, you cause a tremor. All those in your vicinity must win a Static Physical Challenge against your Physical Traits or be knocked to the ground for one minute.

Taking the Skin

By slaying a creature and expending a Mental Trait, you subsume the Beast-nature of your victim. Doing so allows you to transform yourself into the creature for the remainder of the night. In order for this power to work, your victim must be a predator of some sort, and must have at least one Blood Trait's worth of vitae — no ants or mosquitoes are permitted.

Upon completion of the proper preparations, you transform physically into your victim and gain its appearance, Physical Traits and abilities. (**Note**: The full effect only takes if the victim is a "natural" creature. *Taking the Skin* of a Lupine or other vampire, for example, only grants you the victim's appearance.)

Appendix

Taken Skins

Some standard shapes taken for transformation include:

Shape	Traits Gained	Other Powers
Hawk:	*Dextrous* and *Graceful*	Flight
Leopard:	*Quick* x3	Claws capable of Aggravated Damage
Bear:	*Resilient* x2, *Tough*, *Vigorous*	

Ogham

Master

Dragon Lines

By spending a Willpower Trait, you can inscribe powerful runes on your body, which becomes a channel for mystic energy for the duration of a single night. Once the power is in effect, you may spend a Mental Trait to retest any challenge directed at you. The only caveat is that your feet must be in contact with bare soil or uncarved stone at the time — flagstones or other trappings of civilization negate this Discipline's effects.

Inscribe the Forgotten Names

You now know the names of some of the monstrous beasts that once walked the Earth, and by using their names you can summon them to you. By succeeding in a Static Social challenge (difficulty at Narrator's discretion — dragons should be much harder to conjure than, say, an oracular pig) you can summon some mythic beast. The beast's powers and temperament are determined by the narrator. Just because you summon the creature doesn't mean it's necessarily friendly. Furthermore, you have no control over the creature you summon, so using this power is risky at best. *Inscribe the Forgotten Names* may be used only once per session.

Deimos

Master

Clutching the Shroud

By drinking the blood from a corpse you may access some of the powers of the Restless Dead. Once you have consumed five Blood Traits of dead blood, you may use that blood for one of the following purposes:

- You may peer into the Shadowlands for up to five minutes per Blood Trait expended. This will let you see wraiths and any other denizens of the Underworld, but will not give you the ability to communicate with them.

- You have the ability to determine the relative health of anyone you see, mimicking the ghostly ability *Lifesight*. While this power is in effect, others must tell you how many wounds they have and how many Blood Traits are currently in their systems. If you see a mortal, you are able to determine if he suffers from any disease or illness. You gain this insight for 10 minutes per Blood Trait expended.

- The last use of this power is the most visibly macabre. By expending all five Blood Traits, your skin hardens as though under the effects of rigor mortis. You are immune to wound penalties and gain the additional Physical Trait *Resilient* x 2 for the remainder of the night.

Lilith's Summons

Your blood may now be smelled in the world of the dead. By spitting a Blood Trait on a target, you "mark" that target, causing Spectres to arrive and seek out the individual for their own unholy enjoyment. By spending a Blood Trait, you may also summon a Spectre to you and communicate with it, though you do not gain any control over the Spectre called. For details on Spectres, see **Oblivion**.

Mortis

Master

Sense Death's Imminence

You may now detect sudden ebbs of life energy when things die. By succeeding in an Extended Static Mental Challenge versus a difficulty determined by the Narrator, you are able to discern the way death has affected places and people.

1 success — You may sense if death has occurred nearby.

2 successes — You are able to discern the basic cause of death.

3 successes — You know the general location and some minor specifics as to the cause of death.

4 successes — You know the specific location and a very strong idea of the events that took place surrounding the death.

5 successes — You can see through the eyes of death itself with crystal clarity and know exactly what happened.

Appendix

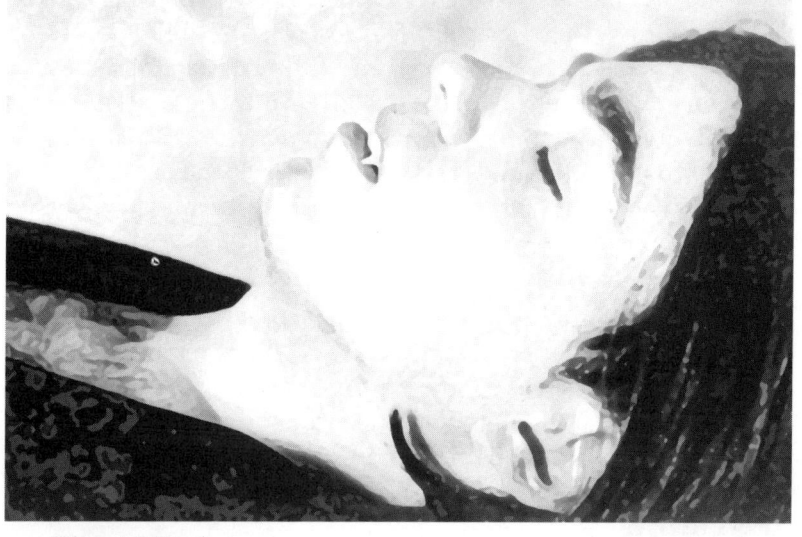

Plague Wind

Similar to the Advanced power *Black Death*, you are now able to unlock the decay in everything around you. By touching a target and expending two Willpower Traits, you cause humans and animals to become infected with a deadly plague. The infected target takes one aggravated wound every 30 minutes until death occurs. Cainites thus infected must defeat you in a Mental Challenge or fall into torpor. Cainites who succeed will not sicken, but are now plague carriers and will spread the disease when they feed. Their "carrier" status lasts for the next three days.

Valeren

Master

Warding the Beast (Healer)

With this power you are to pull the soul of another and take it into your own body, where powerful healing magic can be worked upon it. To activate this power you must defeat the target, if he is unwilling, in a Mental Challenge (though no challenge is required to affect a willing target). Upon doing so you are able to expend one temporary Willpower Trait to restore a Trait of the soul's Via rating. While you have control of the soul within you, the body is a mindless shell without motavation or free will. If the body is destroyed the soul immediately vanishes

and you automatically lower your Via rating by three. The souls of these Cainites become Spectres as described in **MET: Oblivion**. This power will not work under the following conditions: the target has a Via rating of one, or is a follower of Via Diabolis. You may only use this power once in the targets lifetime. To keep a soul for too long is heinous and cruel. For every day past the first that you keep the target's soul in your body you must lower your Via rating by one.

Loving Agony (Warrior)

Your touch now causes pain and actual damage to your enemies. With the expenditure of a Willpower Trait (and a Physical Challenge to touch your target if he is not immobile), you may do one non-Aggravated wound per Blood Trait spent. Due to the unbearable pain, a Cainite that takes more wounds in this manner than he has Willpower Traits automatically enters frenzy.

Safe Passage (Healer)

Safe Passage is similar to the Presence power *Majesty*, but functions in a much more passive way. Someone who wishes to harm you must first defeat you in a Mental Challenge; if he fails, he not only forgets why he was attempting to hurt you, but also finds reasons to avoid you for the remainder of the evening. This power only works on casual acquaintances and strangers, as those who know you well will be able to overcome the suggestion of non-aggression. Once learned, this power is always active.

Aversion (Warrior)

You are now able to make others seem unlikeable. By touching the target and expending a Blood Trait, you grant him the following Negative Traits for the remainder of the night: *Repugnant* x 2 and *Callous* x 2. The victim must act out these Traits once they have been installed, though he has no idea where they came from.

In addition, you can use *Aversion* to get others to attack your target. At your discretion, you may engage in a Mental Challenge with anyone you choose. If you win, you can "suggest" that the loser attack the target of *Aversion*. The "attacker" will rationalize assaulting the victim as her own idea, perhaps even making up a story for the sheriff about something the victim did to her.

Appendix

FAQ

Am I able to spend a Willpower Trait to attempt to detect an Obfuscated entity passing by?

No. You can't use your Willpower Trait to negate the effects of the another's *Obfuscate*.

Is a character limited in the number of times she may spend Willpower (up to the character's current maximum) to re-enter her body if someone with Necromancy successfully removes her soul from it?

No. Home is where the heart is (not to mention the liver, lungs, kidneys...).

Can I transfer my experience between characters?

The polite answer to this one is, "Are you out of your freakin' gourd?" No, players may not transfer experience from character to character! Jarl the Gangrel learned his lesson that night; there's no reason Winslow the Ventrue should benefit even if the same player stands behind both. The only time a Storyteller should allow a player to create a new character with experience to spend is in the case of a "good death" — usually one accepted for the benefit of the chronicle as a whole.

If the character lived by her own code (the player portrayed her Nature and Demeanor well), and the character went out in an appropriate fashion, the supervising Narrator may allow the player to apply that game's experience award to her next character. These awards can't be "saved up," though, and once you have a bonus like that on the books, you can't gain another until the previous one is spent. Simply put, you can't use multiple experience awards to create a godlike starting character.

What is the maximum number of experience points I can gain?

This up to your individual troupe, but we recommend no more than six experience points per month of fairly active gameplay. You shouldn't be going from warm snack to elder too quickly, after all.

What is the maximum amount of experience I can receive at one time?

Players can receive up to three experience points per game session.

How does damage work in regard to causing Final Death?

If a Kindred suffers sufficient aggravated damage to reduce her past the "Torpor" Health Level, she dies the Final Death. Note that

all the damage she has suffered need not be aggravated; the last one is the one that matters.

What is the range of Mental and Social Disciplines?

All Mental and Social Disciplines are limited to direct unaided line of sight (no bionoculars, periscopes, telescopes, etc.), unless otherwise stated. Storytellers should, of course, feel free to play with this limitation when the story demands.

How long do characters stay in torpor?

Once in torpor, characters sleep for two weeks per Beast/Path Trait they possess, though the sleep can be longer for older Cainites — anything that knocks a Methuseleh into torpor packs a helluva wallop. Vampires awakening from torpor do so in a state of blood frenzy, and must feed immediately.

How often does my character replenish his Traits?

Physical, Social and Mental Traits are recovered in full after the character has had at least eight hours of sleep. For gameplay purposes, this means the next night of play unless something goes horribly wrong.

*How long is a **MET** session?*

A session is defined as one period of play for a game of **Mind's Eye Theatre**, usually lasting for an evening. A story's ending is determined by the Storyteller, though having four to six sessions per story is common. It is usually considered ended when the majority of plot devices have been accomplished. When the rules state that something is returned or replenished at the end of the story, it is strictly a Storyteller decision as to when this occurs.

My vampire character has a Garou Fetish that requires Gnosis to activate. Is there any way can I activate its powers?

Short of giving it to a werewolf, no.

Can non-Assamite blood wake Assamites from torpor?

No, it cannot. Non-Assamite vitae is poison to clan members, and if ingested into their system it causes damage as normal. Assamite *antitribu* blood can bring clan members out of torpor, but no other vampires' blood can.

Can Assamites commit diablerie?

No, they cannot. Assamites gain no benefit from Kindred vitae whatsoever. Only Assamite *antitribu* can commit traditional diablerie.

Appendix

Can Nectar of the Bitter Rose be used multiple times from the same victim (if a 13th generation Kindred drinks all five draughts from a seventh-generation victim, can he be lowered to eighth generation)?

Absolutely not. One shot and then you're done, kiddo.

Can a blood draught from Nectar of the Bitter Rose be stored for later consumption?

No. The draught of blood must be consumed at the time of the ritual or it goes rancid.

My character has Vicissitude. When will he get taken over by a Souleater?

It depends. If you think the Black Hand is full of it, Souleaters aren't a concern.

If you do believe in Souleaters, the answer is still "Never ever ever." Souleaters are Narrator characters, and should never be handed over to players. Characters with *Vicissitude* never metamorphose into Souleaters unless the player relinquishes the character to a Narrator.

What Disciplines can be used while one is staked?

None. Having a stick through your sternum limits your flexibility of response.

What Disciplines can be used in conjunction with Celerity?

Animalism: Embrace the Beast, Conquer the Beast

Fortitude: All

Potence: All

Presence: Majesty

Protean: All

Serpentis: The Serpent's Tongue

Spiritus: Aspect of the Beast, The Wildebeast, Spirit Form

Vicissitude: Horrid Form, Body Arsenal, Plasmic Form

Visceratika: Stonestrength, Rockheart

Note: *Plasmic Form* may not be activated while one is using *Celerity*, but if it has already been activated, it may be used as normal.

What is the effect of having zero (0) Blood Traits?

For Kindred, blood frenzy (assuming that you have the *Hunger Beast Trait*). For mortals, revenants, ghouls and Garou, death.

When a character learns Eyes of the Serpent do her eyes permanently change appearance?

No.

When I use Spiritus, Necromancy or Spirit Thaumaturgy, are the spirits summoned Umbral nature spirits or wraiths?

Spiritus only summons Umbral nature spirits. *Necromancy* summon wraiths. *Spirit Thaumaturgy* is usually used on Umbral spirits, but may function on wraiths at the Storyteller's option.

Laws of the Night FAQ Clarifications

If the target of Beast Within does not have any Derangements, what happens?

If the target has no Derangements, then *Beast Within* affects Beast/Path Traits. If she has no Derangements or Beast/Path Traits, nothing happens.

While using Possession, can I use the host body's Disciplines?

All Physical Disciplines (*Celerity, Fortitude, Potence, Vicissitude, Visceratika*) stay with the body possessed and the possessor may use them. All other Disciplines are linked to mental ability and knowledge, and as such, the possessor cannot use them. Of course, you can take your mental Disciplines with you when you skip bodies.

What happens when a Kindred with Majesty meets a Kindred with Majesty?

The Kindred with the lower generation's *Majesty* takes precedence. If both Kindred are of the same generation, their powers cancel one another out and they react normally.

What happens if I am using Possession and the body I'm in is killed?

If you are currently possessing another Kindred, you die. If you are possessing a mortal (ghouls do count as mortal), you revert back to your normal body, minus half your current Willpower Traits. These Traits are not lost permanently, and may be regained at a rate of one per night.

Laws of Elysium

Negative Traits

Mental Traits

Social Traits

Physical Traits

Status

Disciplines

Abilities

Merits **Flaws**

Beast Traits / Path Traits

Willpower
○ ○ ○ ○ ○ ○ ○ ○ ○ ○
☐ ☐ ☐ ☐ ☐ ☐ ☐ ☐ ☐ ☐

Blood
○ ○ ○ ○ ○ ○ ○ ○ ○ ○
☐ ☐ ☐ ☐ ☐ ☐ ☐ ☐ ☐ ☐

Influences

Derangements

Player_____
Character_____
Chronicle_____
Nature_____
Demeanor_____
Concept_____
Clan_____
Generation_____
Haven_____
Experience_____
Age_____

Laws of Elysium

Index

A

Abilities 20
Acquired Tastes 30
Advantages 20
Age of Consideration 35
All-Elder Chronicle 124
Attributes 20
Avoiding Unnecessary Violence 114

B

Beast/Path Traits 22, 47
Blood Addiction 145
Blood Expenditures 146
Blood Storage 146
Blood Traits 21
Blood Traits of Food Source 146

C

Caitiff 44
Camarilla 39
Character Advancement 140
Character Creation
  Chart 18
  Example of 23
  Name 19
Clans 40
  Assamite 42
  Brujah 40
  Daughters of Cacophony 42
  Followers of Set 42
  Gangrel 40
  Giovanni 42
  Lasombra 44
  Malkavians 40
  New 45
    Dark Ages Gargoyles 46
    Gargoyles 45
    Lasombra *Antitribu* 46
    Old Clan Tzimisce 47
  Nosferatu 41
  Ravnos 43
  Salubri 43
  Samedi 43
  Toreador 41
  Tremere 41
  Tzimisce 44
  Ventrue 41
Costuming 106

D

Defining the Role 96
Disciplines 21, 59
  Abombwe 148
    Devil-Channel 148
    Taking the Skin 148
  Animalism 60
    Animal Succulence 60
    Conquer the Beast 60
  Auspex 61
    Clairvoyance 61
    Soul Scan 61
  Bardo 61
    Bring Forth the Dawn 61
  Celerity 62
    Quickness 62
    Velocity 62
  Chimerstry 62
    Fata Morgana 62
    Mass Reality 63
    Pseudo Blindness 62
  Deimos 149
    Clutching the Shroud 149
    Lilith's Summons 150
  Dementation 63
    Kindred Spirits 63
    Mind of a Killer 63
  Dominate 64
    Obedience 64
    Rationale 64
  Fortitude 64
    Imperviousness 64
    Invulnerability 64
  Melpominee 64
    Art's Traumatic Essence 65
    Earth Sword 66
    The Missing Voice 64
  Mortis 150
    Plague Wind 151
    Sense Death's Imminence 150
  Mytherceria 65
    Darkling Trickery 65
    Riddle Phantastique 65
  Necromancy 66
    Insight 66
    Spirit Possession 66
    Torment 66
  Obeah 67
    Anesthetic Touch 67
    Pain for Pleasure 67
    Vitae Block 67
  Obfuscate 67
    Cloak the Aura 67
    Conceal 68
  Obtenebration 68
    Eyes of the Night 68
    Shadow Step 68
  Ogham 149
    Dragon Lines 149
    Inscribe the Forgotten Names 149
  Potence 69
    Demolition 69
    Force 69
  Presence 69
    Love 69
    Mind Numb 69
  Protean 70
    Flesh of Marble 70
    Form of the Ghost 70
  Quietus 70
    Foul Blood 71
    Taste of Death 70
    Weakness 70
  Serpentis 71
    Obsession 71
    Temptation 71
  Spiritus 71
    Engling Fury 72
    Spirit Form 72
    Summon Spirit Beasts 71

Index

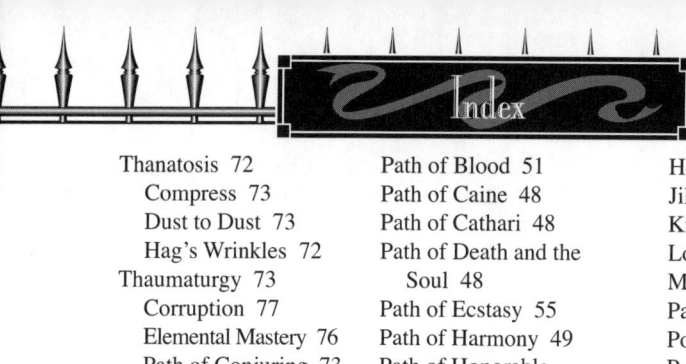

Thanatosis 72
  Compress 73
  Dust to Dust 73
  Hag's Wrinkles 72
Thaumaturgy 73
  Corruption 77
  Elemental Mastery 76
  Path of Conjuring 73
  Spirit Thaumaturgy 74
Valeren 151
  Aversion 152
  Loving Agony 152
  Safe Passage 152
  Warding the Beast 151
Vicissitude 78
  Body Arsenal 78
  Plasmic Form 78
Viscertika 79
  Bond with Terra 79
  Rockheart 80
  Skin of the Chameleon 79
  Stonestrength 80
  Voices of the Castle 79
  Whispers of the Chamber 79

E

Elders 12
Experience 141
  Chart 142
  Time-lapse Advancement 143

F

FAQ 153
  Laws of the Night 156

G

Gehenna Cults 37
Generation 21
Golconda 35

H

Harbingers of Doom 98
Hierarchy of Sins 48

Path of Blood 51
Path of Caine 48
Path of Cathari 48
Path of Death and the Soul 48
Path of Ecstasy 55
Path of Harmony 49
Path of Honorable Accord 49
Path of Humanity 49
Path of Paradox 52
Path of Power and the Inner Voice 50
Path of the Warrior 56
Path of Typhon 54

I

Independents 42
Influence 26
  Mortal Allies 118
Influences 21, 26
  Bureaucracy 26
  Church 26
  Finance 26
  Health 27
  High Society 27
  Industry 27
  Legal 28
  Media 28
  Occult 28
  Police 28
  Politics 29
  Street 29
  Transportation 29
  Underworld 29
  University 29

L

Long Night, The 148

M

Merits and Flaws 31
  Appropriate 31
  New 31
    Bastard Childe 31
    Death Wish 33
    Enlightened 34

    Holdings 33
    Jilted Paramour 33
    Known Diablerist 32
    Loyal Childe 32
    Matricide/Patricide 32
    Paramour 34
    Poverty 31
    Prestation Debt 33
    Prestation Gifts 34
    Recently Arisen 32
    Secret Diablerist 32
    Vainglorious 33
    Vengeful Childe 31
Mind's Eye Theatre 12

P

Paths 47
  Clan-Specific 50
  Path of Blood 50
  Path of Ecstasy 55
  Path of Paradox 52
  Path of the Warrior 56
  Path of Typhon 54
Prestation 120
Pretenders 142

R

Rituals 80
  Antitribu 87
    Bottled Voice 90
    Craft Bloodstone 89
    Dominion 92
    Eldritch Glimmer 90
    Eyes of the Beast 92
    Eyes of the Nighthawk 88
    Fire Walker 90
    Friend of the Trees 90
    Illuminate Trail of the Prey 88
    Impassable Trail 88
    Keening of the Banshee 91
    Lion Heart 92
    Machine Blitz 88
    Mindcrawler 92
    Mirror Walk 91
    Paper Flesh 93

Power of the Invisible Flame 89
Preserve Blood 89
Respect of the Animals 91
Steps of the Terrified 89
Summon Guardian
Spirit of Torment 93
The Haunting 90
Touch of Nightshade 91
Will o' the Wisp 89
Assamite 86
   Blood Call 86
   Blood of Peace 86
   Healing Blood 87
   Light of Vengeance 86
Binding the Beast 82
Bladed Hands 82
Blood Contract 85
Blood Walk 80
Calling the Restless Spirit 80
Curse of Clytaemnestra 85
Donning the Mask of Shadows 80
Eyes of the Past 83
Flesh of Fiery Touch 83
Gentle Mind 83
Haunted House 83
Heart of Stone 83
Illusion of Peaceful Death 84
Innocence of the Child's Heart 84
Mourning Life Curse 81
Principal Focus of Vitae Infusion 81
Protean Curse 84
Rebirth of Mortal Vanity 81
Rending Sweet Earth 84
Rite of Introduction 81
Scent of the Garou's Passing 82
Stone Slumber 85
The Open Passage 82
The Unseen Change 85
The Watcher 85
Wake with Morning's (Evening's) Freshness 82
Roleplaying 95
   Creating an Elder Character 99
   Effective 105
   Elder Motivations 101
   Elder Perspectives 100
   Establishing Alliances 112
   Interacting with Ancillae 111
   Interacting with Elders 114
   Interacting with Neonates 109
   Responsible 99
Rules
   Blood 145
   Clarifications 145
   Important 13
   New 145
   Willpower 147

S

Sabbat 43
Snide Commentary 115
Status 21
Storytelling 123
   Characters 126
   Elder Plot Hooks 135
   Example of 131
   Integrating Elders into a Regular Chronicle 132
   Plot 128
   Scale 124
   Scope 125
   Theme 130
Symbols of Authority 95

T

Trait Maximums 34
Troubleshooting 136

W

Willpower 21, 147
   Frenzy 147
   Ignoring Wounds 147
   Replenishing 147
   Replenishing Traits With 147
   Staying Awake 147